Samantha Rite Mystery Series Book 1

Hope Callaghan

FIRST EDITION

hopecallaghan.com

Copyright © 2014
All rights reserved.

Visit my website for new releases and special offers: hopecallaghan.com

TABLE OF CONTENTS

Prologue

He stood staring down at the petite blonde sprawled out on the bed. He never meant to kill her. It was all her fault. If she'd just shut up - but she didn't. She went on and on about the money. How she was going to spend her share. The trips to Europe, the designer clothes, the new sports car. And then she said something else. The one thing that she shouldn't have.

She told her sister about the job. About the money. After that, he knew he had to kill her. She couldn't keep her mouth shut. He could no longer trust her.

Dumb broad. Now he'd have to find someone else. And fast.

He opened the slider and stepped out onto the balcony. He lit a cigarette and took a deep drag. Now he had another problem. What to do with the body.

He had been very careful to avoid the hotel cameras. No one had seen him come in and no one would see him go out. He glanced back towards the room. She wasn't scheduled to check out until tomorrow. By then he'd be long gone.

He dropped the cigarette on the cement floor and crushed it out before tossing it over the balcony to the ground below.

He walked back inside to take care of the small details. After carefully wiping the door knobs, the toilet handle and the TV remote, he grabbed his backpack and slung it across his shoulder.

With one last glance at the motionless woman on the bed, he grabbed the *Do Not Disturb* sign off the wall and carefully placed it in the holder on the outside of the door.

After checking to make sure it was shut, he sauntered down the hallway and into the elevator.

Chapter 1

Samantha shook her head as she peered inside her daughter's trunk. It was crammed full of junk – empty water bottles, fast food wrappers, wadded up clothes, a tennis racket. There was even a picnic basket. After a couple of turns this way and that, she was able to wedge her suitcase inside and barely close the lid.

Huge, wet snowflakes quickly coated the top of Sam's head, creating a white halo. The snow was really coming down! She cast a wary eye skyward. *What a great day to leave on a warm, sunny vacation.*

Her feet skidded on an icy patch as she gingerly shuffled her way to the passenger side door. Without taking the time to kick the snow off her favorite leather boots, she jumped into the seat and buckled herself in. She bent over to wipe them dry as Brianna cautiously backed the car out of the driveway.

"You really need to clean out your car – I could hardly get the trunk closed!"

Her daughter rolled her eyes. "Yes, Mom. I'm going to get to it." Here came the excuses. "I've been trying to squeeze it in when I'm not in school or at work but the weather has been crappy ..."

Good one. Laying on the guilt. Sam ignored her answer. "Do you know you have a picnic basket in there???"

Brianna giggled as she shook her head. "I'll have it cleaned out before I pick you up next week. I promise."

Sam switched her attention to the weather outside. The roads were covered in snow and ice. The streets were becoming more treacherous by the minute as it began snowing even harder. Sam peered out the window. It looked as if they were inside a giant snow globe that had just been shaken. With every passing mile, Sam worried that Brianna's trip back home would be dangerous.

The weather in Michigan could change in an instant when winter storms blew across the Great Lakes. It looked like this one was going to be a doozy.

Brianna read her mother's mind. "Mom, don't worry. I'll be fine. We aren't really that far from the airport and I'll take the back roads home."

Sam smiled over at Brianna. "Yes, I'm sure you will." Her daughter knew her all too well.

Brianna was the most precious thing in Sam's life. At 22 years old, her whole life was ahead of her. She was finishing her degree in marketing and interning full time at a local ad agency.

Brianna was a pretty girl with a heart-shaped face, long blonde hair and sparkling blue eyes. She had her mother's shape - petite and on the thin side.

Over the years, Sam watched the boyfriends come and go. She had really liked some of them but none lasted very long. The longest was a year. Bri, as she was called, knew exactly what she wanted. She just hadn't found him yet.

Born and raised in West Michigan, Bri was tired of living here. To her, it was one of the most boring places on earth. Unless you liked hunting. Or fishing. Or snow. She definitely didn't like the snow. The long, cold, dreary winters dragged on forever. There were very few sunny days and when the sun did shine, it practically blinded you when it bounced off the pure white snowdrifts. No, she did not like living in Michigan at all.

But Brianna had been working on her mother. Wearing her down, really. She wanted to move somewhere warmer – and she was convinced her mom should go with her. Since her parent's recent divorce, finally finishing school and gearing up to embark on a new career, she was certain her mom would follow.

Sam was an insurance agent and the agency she worked for had locations all over the U.S. She could easily transfer to any one of them if she wanted to. At least that was Brianna's reasoning.

She had narrowed her search down to California, Atlanta or Orlando. California would probably be super-expensive, Atlanta too crowded with too much traffic. Warm weather, beaches and fun stuff to do topped Brianna's list and she'd almost decided that Florida would be perfect. Maybe it wasn't fair, but Bri knew that if she told her mom she was serious about moving, her mom would more than likely go with her.

Although their entire family lived in Michigan, nothing was really keeping them here any longer. After the divorce, Bri's dad rarely called her and she was fine with that. He had his new wife and his new life now so he didn't need her anymore.

It was another ten minutes of white knuckle driving before they finally pulled up in front of the Grand Rapids International Airport.

Sam grabbed the door handle and pushed her way out into the blustery cold. Despite the hazardous weather, the airport unloading area was bustling.

Sam pulled her suitcases from the trunk of the car and shook her head as she looked at the inside. She impulsively grabbed an empty shopping bag and started throwing handfuls of trash into it.

"Mom, *what* are you doing?" Brianna was now standing beside her mom, hands on her hips.

"I'm giving you a head start!" She grabbed an empty Kleenex box just before her daughter pushed her away and slammed the lid shut.

"Stop! I promise it'll be spotless the next time you see it!"

Sam nodded. Maybe she was just nervous. Cleaning always seemed to make her feel calmer.

The moment she was practically dreading was at hand. There was nothing left to do but head inside. She straightened her back, squared her shoulders and hugged her only child. Trying to appear braver than she felt, she marched off into the airport terminal.

"See you next week. Don't forget to pick me up." Sam called out behind her as she made her way through the sliding glass doors.

Check-in was fast and soon she was navigating the long line through security. By the time she reached the gate, passengers were already boarding.

Wow, we cut that a little close, Sam thought.

She pushed her carry-on bag under the seat and settled in next to the window. A frown crossed her face as she gazed out at the huge snowflakes that were still coming down.

The last time she was in Miami was with Anthony. They spent a long, romantic weekend in South Beach. That trip had been a perfect escape – just the two of them. Looking back, she wondered if the trip was as magical as she remembered or if he had just been really good at faking it.

Sam's brow furrowed. The happy memories were quickly crowded out by the bad and she started to feel depressed. *Had he ever really loved her or was it all an act? If he had loved her, when did he stop?*

Pushing the thoughts of her cheating ex-husband out of her mind was hard but Sam was determined. This vacation was about getting away and forgetting all the horrible crap she'd gone through this past year. Anthony's betrayal, his admitted affair with one of the partners in his real estate office, the shame she felt. The hardest part of all was the pity she saw in the eyes of her friends and family when the whole horrible affair and inevitable divorce unfolded for all the world to see.

The sadness and pain of it all were just too much. Unexpected tears welled up in her eyes. She quickly wiped them away as she glanced around, hoping no one witnessed her small meltdown.

Sam's support group had saved her sanity during and after the ugly divorce. She started the group at her church years ago after she was unexpectedly diagnosed with cancer. When she shared the news with a few of her closest friends, one of them encouraged her to create the small group – a kind-of support system to help each other deal with life changing events.

When she really thought about it, she realized Anthony was little help after her cancer diagnosis. She tried to open up about her fears or ask his advice on decisions that needed to be made. His only response was to abruptly shut down and change the subject.

She practically pleaded with him to go with her for a doctor visit or chemo appointment but he always had an excuse. He never did go – not even once.

Her family had their own lives to deal with and she didn't want to be a burden. There was no one to turn to.

Over the years, the group had taken on a life of its own. Now one of the largest groups in her church, it consisted mostly of women – from young Twentysomethings to Great-Grandmas. Everyone was facing a different battle - from divorce to death to life-threatening illnesses to a job loss. When she started it, she had no idea how many hurting people there were – right in her own back yard.

With the help of the support group, someone was there to go with her when she went in for surgery and then for her chemotherapy and endless radiation treatments. Oftentimes, more than one person would offer to take her.

After the chemo treatments, Sam was completely wiped out. It would take days to recover. Lying in bed, sick and tired was the only thing she could do. Time after time, someone from the group would show up on her doorstep with cooked meals or bags of groceries. More importantly, they were always there with love and support.

Nighttime was the worst for Sam. So many nights she would lay in bed, wide awake. In those long, still hours, the terrifying thoughts would slowly creep in. No matter how many times the doctors reassured her she had a promising outlook for full recovery and a long life still ahead of her, the word

11

cancer filled her mind. Cancer and death. The two just seemed to go together.

Those were some very dark days and Sam thanked God every day for the prayer warriors, for caring friends, and for her own eternal salvation. Even in the deepest, darkest places, she always felt God's love and peace.

"To be absent from the body is to be present with the Lord." *2 Corinthians 5:8 KJV*

She would constantly remind herself of this verse. If she died, there was no doubt she would be in heaven.

She would be forever grateful for those friends that took the long, terrifying journey with her and held her hand the entire way.

Looking back now, she wasn't sure if cancer was the worst thing she'd gone through – or the heartbreaking betrayal of the man she loved so deeply and trusted without question.

Chapter 2

Standing on the balcony outside his hotel room, Lee Windsor looked blankly into the distance, wishing he was anywhere but here. Admittedly, the Florida weather was gorgeous. A gentle breeze blew through the Royal palm trees circling the courtyard pool.

Now would be a good time to smoke a cigarette, Lee thought to himself. He quit that nasty habit a few years back and was glad that he had. Except for times like these.

Most would describe Lee as the quiet type. Women were attracted to him like a moth to a flame. They were always trying to break through the impenetrable wall he built around him.

Lee was definitely easy on the eyes. At almost 6' tall, he had broad shoulders and a narrow waist. Even a passing glance revealed his almost flawless physique. His blonde hair was cut very short but the style suited his rugged good looks.

His most striking feature by far was his piercing eyes. They were the most incredible shade of emerald green. And if they focused on you long enough, it was as if he could see in to your soul.

Annie would've loved this whole adventure. He could see her now – the look of excitement and anticipation on her face as she soaked it all in – the warm sunshine, gently-swaying palm trees, a romantic evening walk on the beach. He slowly shook his head. Why hadn't he ever taken the time to surprise her with a place like this? But it was too late now - he would never get the chance.

Annie was like a magnet and people were always drawn to her. At first glance, it would seem they sought her out for her natural beauty – the long blonde, naturally-curly hair, her crystal-clear blue eyes, but no – it was definitely her smile that drew them in. When Annie smiled, the whole room would light up. Even the most ill-tempered person would smile back when Annie turned on her charm. And she was just so genuine. She didn't have a mean bone in her body. No matter how irritating or annoying someone was, she always saw the best in them – and she had a way of bringing that best out.

Annie looked at life as the glass half full. She was never down. Everything she did and everywhere she went was a great adventure. Around every corner was something new to discover or somewhere new to explore. Lee had never met anyone quite like her. He was sure he probably never would again.

For a moment, Lee allowed himself to wallow in his own self-pity, his eyes burning from years of unshed tears. He was missing Annie fiercely. His heart was breaking – for the thousandth time. If only he could have just one more day with her, one more hour ...

Bleep! Bleep! A car alarm started blaring in the parking lot below and reality came crashing in. He lifted his head and swallowed hard. With his mouth drawn in a straight and angry line, he turned on his heel and walked back into the hotel room, slamming the slider door shut behind him.

Chapter 3

Two hours later, Sam's plane safely landed in Miami, much to her relief. She never did care much for flying and flying solo was even worse. At least traveling with someone took her mind off her claustrophobia – and her fear of crashing.

As soon as she was able, Sam checked her phone and was relieved when she listened to Brianna's message, letting her know she had made it home safely and that the weather was getting worse.

She grabbed her bags from the carousel and made her way outside the terminal. The warm sunshine enveloped her. Palm trees lined the sidewalk and a gentle breeze was blowing. She closed her eyes for a second, soaking in the sun and welcoming the heat.

It didn't take long to flag down a cab to take her to her hotel, the Miami Intracoastal on beautiful Biscayne Bay. She originally booked this hotel because she thought she and her sister would have fun catching up and getting excited about their first-ever cruise they would be embarking on the next day.

Part of this trip was supposed to be a celebration of Sam's 40th birthday and the start of a new chapter in her life. The last decade had been rough to say the least. She was looking forward to leaving the bad behind and starting over.

Everything changed when her sister, Deb, fell off her 4-wheeler on her property in Northern Michigan the week before. Not only did she break two of her ribs, but she suffered a serious concussion. Sam sighed. *When she did something, she did it right!*

After spending a couple nights in the hospital, it was obvious that Deb would not be going anywhere anytime soon and she certainly wouldn't be making this trip. Sam was deeply disappointed.

Even though her aunt wasn't able to take the cruise, Brianna convinced her mom to go alone. Bri tried hard to figure out some way she could go with her since the trip was already paid for, but she was in the midst of final exams. There was really no way she could take a vacation right now.

She knew her mother was in desperate need of this break. The heartbreak and pain from the past year – actually the past decade - had taken its toll. Her mom looked so sad and tired all the time. She looked beaten and it was a look that Brianna wasn't used to seeing. Brianna was finally able to wear her down and convince her to go. Looking back now, Sam was glad she did.

After a short taxi ride, they pulled up in front of the hotel. Her bags were quickly unloaded. She paid the taxi driver and made her way into the hotel lobby. It was absolutely stunning – so stunning, it almost took her breath away. The fabulous grand lobby consisted of Italian marble slabs and precious African wood. The lobby's centerpiece was an 18 foot tall, 70-ton round sculpture. The sculpture was made of solid marble. A sparkling waterfall cascaded over the centerpiece and flowed into a surrounding crystal-clear pool.

The hotel was the epitome of elegance; *beautiful, simply beautiful*, Sam thought. From the 36-story marble exterior to the soaring atrium. Sam soaked it all in as she reminded herself she made the right decision, even if she was by herself.

Check-in was a breeze and before she knew it, she was standing inside her spacious guestroom. The bathroom was spa-luxurious, complete with granite counters, marble floors and a deep, jetted tub. The spacious glass shower was huge. There had to be room for a dozen people in there! Sam peeked inside. Even that was marble!

The room was perfect and Sam was *not* going to let the fact that she was alone in a strange city, about to embark on a vacation with thousands of people she'd never met keep her from having fun!

She hurriedly changed into one of her new sundresses and walked over to the mirror to inspect. Sam gazed critically at her reflection in the mirror. She liked to think of herself as petite – not short – coming in at a mere 5'3". Because of her height, she forever had to watch her weight. That was a problem lately. Since the divorce, Sam lost 20 lbs. and most of her old clothes no longer fit.

She and Bri recently spent the day shopping, picking out some new clothes for her to bring along. The wardrobe they picked out were mostly things that her daughter liked. Sam herself would never have chosen some of the outfits, but now that the dress was on, she had to admit it made her look younger than her 40 years.

She spent the last year letting her dark brown hair grow out. Her favorite style was pulled back into a long, elegant ponytail. Quick and easy.

Personally, she didn't think she possessed any striking features. Hazel eyes, a pert nose and an oval face would be an accurate description. Everyone told her she had a nice smile. She hadn't done much of that lately but hopefully that was about to change.

She finished freshening up before taking one last look in the mirror. *As ready as I'll ever be*, she decided.

Sam grabbed her room key and purse and headed down to find the hotel's restaurant, Nuevo Latina. The restaurant got excellent on-line reviews for their Pan Latin cuisine and she was excited to try the food.

The restaurant was easy to find and soon she was standing nervously outside the entrance. It was still early. She peeked around the corner. Only a few of the tables were occupied. She took a deep breath and forced herself to step inside.

Her eyes were immediately drawn to the large picture windows and the breathtaking views of the bay. Décor inside was comfortable-looking overstuffed leather furniture complemented by deep cherry wood and dark spindle wrought-iron.

When the hostess discovered she was dining alone, she nodded sympathetically and led Sam to a small table by the window. The bay view was incredible. From where she was sitting, the small sailboats and luxury yachts looked like children's toys.

Grateful she wasn't conspicuously seated in the center of the restaurant, she smiled warmly at the hostess. "Thank you. This table is perfect."

Sam sipped a glass of Chardonnay as she perused the menu. So many intriguing menu items made it difficult to decide!

"Good evening, madam." She looked up to see a tall, smiling waiter standing directly in front of her. "My name is Armand. Do you have any questions about our menu?" he asked.

Sam nodded hesitantly. "I-I have no idea what to order. Everything sounds so tempting," she confessed.

Armand pulled a pad of paper and pen from his pocket. "May I make a suggestion then?"

"Yes, of course! Maybe you could surprise me with one of your favorites?" Sam said.

A beaming smile lit up his face. "Certainly! You won't be sorry!" he assured her.

Sam was still gazing out at the magnificent bay view when he returned a little while later with one of their trademark dishes - Chipotle Chilean Sea Bass accompanied by baby carrots and asparagus with a side of their crispy Truffle Fries.

Sam carefully inspected the dish he set in front of her. "This is perfect, Armand!"

His selection was spot on and she was glad she left it up to him to decide. She savored each bite and finished every single morsel.

Sam was just finishing her meal when Armand returned to the table with a second glass of wine.

Sam shook her head in confusion. "I didn't order another glass."

He carefully set the glass in front of her and then pointed towards the bar. "The gentleman over at the bar ordered this for you," he explained.

Sam quickly glanced in that direction. The bar was empty. "There's no one there."

Armand turned to look for himself. "He was sitting there just a minute ago..." Obviously there was some sort of misunderstanding. "I'll be right back." Armand crossed the restaurant and headed straight to the small bar area on the other side.

He spent several minutes talking to the bartender before returning. "The man told the bartender to send a glass of wine over to the pretty woman by the window that was eating alone."

Sam was puzzled. "And then he just left?"

Armand nodded slowly. "He paid in cash and left right after," he explained.

Sam took a couple sips, just to be polite, before leaving the nearly full glass on the table. Why on earth would someone buy her a drink and then take off before she had a chance to even thank him? She waved goodbye to Armand on her way out.

It was time to check out the rest of the hotel. Sam was amazed at the size of the sparkling blue pool. It was flanked on either side by an outdoor café and separate Tiki bar. She was disappointed to discover neither was open this late in the day.

Too bad I couldn't stay longer, Sam thought. *I would definitely spend some time out here!*

Dozens of lounge chairs lined the edge of the pool and a collection of more intimate sitting areas were spread throughout the patio. There were padded iron chairs, complemented by vibrant-colored umbrellas in tropical shades of lime green and bright, sunny yellow. It looked like the perfect place to relax and indulge in a fruity cocktail. The shimmering bay was a stunning backdrop and could be seen from almost every angle of the pool deck.

Sam spent a few more minutes looking around. By now, it was starting to get dark. There were now only a couple people wandering around. Except for a man who was sitting at a nearby table. He was strangely dressed and looked out of place, wearing a turtle neck sweater and long pants. It was definitely too warm for winter clothes. The other thing that caught her eye was his ball cap. It was pulled way down and he had on a pair of dark sunglasses that hid his eyes. The sun had gone down long ago.

The others on the deck had already gone back inside. Sam and this oddly-dressed man were suddenly the only ones around. The hair on the back of her neck stood up. He was beginning to make her feel a more than a little uneasy.

She glanced around, her eyes lighting on a nearby door leading indoors. She quickly made her way to the entrance. When she got there, she glanced into the reflection of the glass. The odd stranger had gotten out of his chair and was following right behind her.

Sam hesitated for a split second. Now was not the time to go to her room. Instead, she walked in the direction of the main lobby.

When she got there, she slowed her pace and casually strolled around the marble sculpture, as if admiring it.

The stranger followed her into the lobby and was now standing directly across from her, studying the sculpture as well!

A low whisper, the voice of reason bounced around in her head. *You're just being paranoid. No need to overreact!* Still, a small nagging thought in the back of her mind told her you can never be too careful.

Sam spun around and looked behind her. The small lobby gift shop was still open. She slipped inside and headed for the bottled water in the back. The store was filled with lots of goodies. Sam eyed the shelves as she walked by. She certainly didn't need it but the gooey, chocolaty candy bars and home decorating magazines were calling her name. Twenty minutes later, and $20 poorer, she walked back out.

Her eyes immediately scanned the enormous lobby. The man was still standing by the center fountain and he was staring right at her!

Now what do I do? She glanced around nervously, her gaze lighting on the front desk. *Why didn't I think of this earlier?* She quickly walked over to the first person she saw. It was the hotel manager.

From the tag he was wearing, she could see his name was Jason.

He smiled as he looked up. "Good evening. How can I help you?"

Without going into too much detail, she briefly explained the situation. "I-I'm sorry to bother you - but I think I'm being followed." Sam now had his full attention. The manager leaned forward, listening intently.

Sam motioned with a twist of her head. "Do you see the man over by the fountain – the one wearing the sunglasses?" she asked.

He glanced over, then nodded.

"I think he's following me," she whispered in a low voice.

"He does seem to be staring in our direction." Jason paused. "Hold on a second. I'll be right back."

With that, he disappeared around the corner of the reception area. Moments later, he returned to where Sam was anxiously waiting. "Follow me."

No need to ask her twice. She stepped behind the counter as they headed towards the back of the desk area and out of sight. Around the corner was a large wooden door with a coded lock. Without hesitating, Jason punched in a code and swung the door open. He stepped aside and motioned her in. The door quickly closed behind them. Jason pulled on it, making sure it locked.

He looked around and then leaned forward, talking to Sam in a quiet voice. "This is strictly against company policy but I think that person in the lobby is up to no good so I'm taking you back to your room using the hotel's secret elevator."

Sam looked up. Sure enough, directly in front of them was an elevator. She shook her head. *That's pretty cool!*

The doors opened and Sam stepped inside with Jason close behind. After pressing her floor number, the doors shut. Sam turned to face him. "I'm sorry for bothering you. I-I just wasn't sure what that man was up to and didn't want him following me back to my room."

"No problem. You did the right thing. You can never be too careful," Jason reassured her.

He wasn't going to take any chances and escorted her all the way to her hotel room door. She pulled her key card from her purse and inserted it in the slot. The green light flashed and she pushed the door open.

He turned to go and suddenly stopped. "There's no way that guy could have followed us but if you're at all worried, I'll send someone by to check on you later," he offered.

"I'll be fine." She was certain she was now safe. "No need to do that. Thank you for everything." With 36 stories and more than 700 rooms, there was no way the stranger would ever be able to figure out what room was hers! Sam thanked Jason again before stepping inside and shutting the door.

Once inside, she locked and bolted the door. She leaned against it and let out a sigh of relief.

The room was almost pitch black. She realized she'd been in such a hurry to head out for dinner, she hadn't bothered to open the curtains. Big, heavy drapes covered one entire wall. Curious to see what was behind them, she reached up and pulled them all the way back and was instantly rewarded with a spectacular view. The lights from the Miami skyline shimmered and danced across the water.

I would never tire of this view, Sam thought to herself. She gazed out the window for several long moments.

Sheer exhaustion finally took over. Sam was suddenly too tired to even put on her pajamas. She pulled the drapes shut and then crawled into bed, clothes and all.

As she drifted off to sleep, she almost – but not quite - forgot that she was in a very big city, would soon be travelling to unfamiliar places – and that she was all alone ....

Chapter 4

Sam's mind vaguely registered there was a telephone ringing but it certainly didn't sound like her cell phone. *I must be dreaming.*

She put the pillow over her head and tried to ignore the ringing but it wouldn't stop, demanding to be answered.

Suddenly, she remembered she wasn't home and it must be the phone in her hotel room. She quickly sat up and reached over to pick it up.

On the other end of the line was her daughter. Brianna was almost panicky, "Mom, are you OK? I tried calling your cell phone three times and finally called the hotel's front desk. They said you hadn't checked out yet and rang me through."

"I'm fine." Sam yawned loudly, totally unaware of how freaked out her daughter was. "I guess I just didn't hear my cell."

The roles had reversed. It was her daughter's turn to worry. "OK, but next time, turn your ringer up. I was worried sick!" Sam grinned. She felt like a scolded child.

31

After a few minutes of chit-chat and insisting to Brianna that she really was OK, Sam told her she needed to get going.

"I better go. I need to get ready yet. I promise I'll text you when I'm on the ship." It was already almost 9 a.m. She hadn't bothered to set her alarm the night before because she never EVER slept that late!

With a quick "I love you" and "Please be careful," Sam hung up and headed for the shower. A small smile reached Samantha's lips. The phone call from Brianna made her feel much better. It reminded her there was someone who loved her and was concerned about her.

She hadn't mentioned the incident from the night before or the stranger she was sure had been following her. That would only scare Bri. Besides, that weirdo was long gone by now.

In the shower, Sam once again marveled at what a fabulous hotel this was and how her sister was really missing out.

With a sudden surge of excitement, she quickly finished showering and dressed. She dabbed

32

on a little make-up, added a few quick brushes of mascara and pulled her long, dark hair into a ponytail. A little spritz of perfume and she was ready to start the next leg of her adventure!

Finding a taxi outside the hotel was fairly simple and soon they were traveling down Biscayne Boulevard. The port and several cruise ships suddenly came into view. They were massive in size and several stories tall, all lined up in a row.

Sam peered keenly out the window. Her eyes widened in amazement as the ships came into full view. She craned her neck to get a better look. She'd never been on a cruise before - nor had she ever even seen an actual cruise ship up close.

"These things are huge." "How on earth do they get these monstrosities out of such a tight spot?" The taxi driver smiled in the rearview mirror. *Ahhh, another first-time cruiser!*

She was starting to feel a bit overwhelmed. *How on earth will I keep from getting lost once I'm onboard?*

Thankfully, she didn't have time to dwell on it. Soon, her ship, the Caribbean Blue, was in sight. The taxi driver stopped in front of the unloading zone and quickly yanked her luggage from the trunk.

After paying him and tipping the porter who grabbed her bags and tossed them into a huge metal bin, she slowly made her way towards the entrance. *What have I gotten myself into??* Too late now. She took a deep breath and bravely marched forward.

The next hour and a half was spent in a blur. From the porters taking her bags to going through security to checking in and getting her room card, it was a whirlwind of activity. There were people everywhere going in all different directions.

As she stood in the long check-in line she felt a twinge of sadness. She missed her sister. Deb would've easily figured out how to navigate the masses of people and piles of paperwork that needed to be filled out.

Get a grip, Sam sternly told herself. *She's not here and you are so you're going to have to deal with it.*

Just when she thought it was more work than it was worth, she found herself on a long ramp with glass walls leading onto the massive ship's balcony. A few more steps forward and she crossed the threshold for her first glimpse of the impressive interior.

Everywhere she looked, it was glass and brass, elegant and understated. The atrium seemed to go up forever. It was all breathtaking and beautiful. For the first time all day, Sam was convinced she was going to have an amazing vacation. Like a kid on Christmas morning, she couldn't wait to see what was next!

Smiling crew were everywhere. Almost all of them stopped to welcome her aboard. They sounded so sincere. More than one urged her to head up to the Lido deck for lunch. It suddenly dawned on her that she had been in such a hurry this morning, she forgot to eat breakfast. She hadn't even realized she was hungry until just now.

The Lido deck was overflowing with people and they all seemed to know where they were going. She looked around, unsure of what direction she should take.

Just then, a crew member walked over to where she was standing. "Lunch is being served inside the sliding doors over there to your left." When he saw her hesitate, he continued, "But if you want something quick and easy with fewer crowds, you can grab a burger or hotdog right around the corner here on the pool deck."

Sam shook her head in wonder. *Wow, so many choices! I could get used to this.*

After her big dinner the night before, she decided on a garden salad and glass of iced tea from the Grand View Café. She finished eating just in time to hear the ship announcement that cabins were now ready.

Tired of hauling her carry-on bag and laptop around, Sam headed down to check out her room. That was no easy feat. She made several wrong turns and ended up on the wrong floor.

She let out a long sigh and furrowed her brows. She was hopelessly lost. Suddenly, she spotted a phone. She had no idea who she was going to call but maybe someone – anyone – on the other end of the line would be able to help her find her cabin.

Just before she reached the phone, she glanced up. There was a large 3-D deck plan on the wall just as plain as day! Sam walked over to briefly study the layout and moments later realized where she'd gone wrong. Finally, she was on the right track and quickly found her cabin.

She inserted her key card and pushed the heavy door open. At first glance, it seemed very small. Tall closets lined one wall and a door on the opposite side opened to a tiny bathroom that held a very small shower. Although the entire bathroom was small, it had an adequate-sized sink and enough shelves to fit all her stuff.

In the main part of the cabin were two twin beds. A mini sofa and glass coffee table were tucked into the corner on one wall. On the other side was a desk and chair. Just beyond the beds was a sliding glass door that led out to the balcony. She popped her head out the door to look around. It wasn't very big – just large enough to hold two chairs and a little round table.

Wow! I'm not sure Debbie and I would have survived each other if we had to stay in such a small room together for a week!

After a few more minutes of inspecting the room, she decided it wasn't so bad after all. It had plenty of storage and how much time was she really going to spend in her room anyways?

****

Frowning, Lee squinted up at the massive cruise ship. *Forgot my darned sunglasses.*

He probably forgot more than that. Everything he brought (you couldn't really call it packing) was shoved into the backpack he was carrying.

He'd had approximately 24 hours to arrange a flight, find a hotel and book a cabin on this ship. He was lucky he'd even remembered his passport. Never one for spontaneity, his frown deepened.

No sense in dwelling on something you can't change. Lee sighed deeply as he made his way into the cruise terminal.

****

Sam spent the rest of her day attending the mandatory muster drill and working out her new dining arrangements since she was now cruising by herself.

The maître d' convinced her to join a large group for dinner. He patted her hand. "You will enjoy dining with others. No one should eat alone." Secretly, she decided she would try it but if it didn't work out, she wouldn't go back.

After finalizing all her changes on board, Sam ordered a Virgin Pina Colada at the bar on the Lido deck and walked over to the railing for the ship's sail away. As the ship drifted away from the dock, Sam felt all her tension and anxiety disappear. She vowed to truly enjoy this trip, to try new things and maybe even make some new friends.

She stood at the railing long enough to catch a glimpse of popular South Beach. She scowled as she thought of Anthony. She shook her head. He had no place here – on her vacation!

Now was a good time to explore what would be her home for the next week. The main show lounge was grand – a soaring two-story theatre with a large stage. On closer inspection, she noticed it even had an orchestra pit!

Next, she discovered what surely must be the most popular place on the ship. It was a long and expansive stretch of open area lined with shops and restaurants from one end to the other. There was even an ice cream shop with a wine bar next door. It reminded her of a small town main street – only indoors! Large groups of people were swarming about. It seemed to be a favorite hangout, especially with the kids onboard.

The spa and gym rounded out her list of places where she planned to spend some time. She scoped out the gym and then wandered over to the spa which was right beside it.

There was a pile of brochures laying on a table outside the door. She reached over and picked one up. There were lots of different services – and prices. She took a closer look. The list included a seaweed massage, hot oil and warm stone therapy, detox.....

"Can I put you down for a massage?"

Startled, Sam looked up to see a smiling dark-haired lady. She shook her head. "I-I'm just not sure yet." She folded the price sheet and tucked it into her front pocket.

"I'm going to take this with me and come back later...when I'm ready to book," she finished. Truthfully, she had never been to a spa before. It was a bit intimidating and a little overwhelming.

On the way back to her cabin she stumbled upon the Solarium. Excitedly, she looked around. It was so quiet and peaceful – the complete opposite of the Lido deck. An adults-only retreat with glass walls and a retractable glass roof covered the small pool. It reminded Sam of a luxury hotel pool, complete with comfy-looking deck furniture, a bubbling fountain, tropical plants and some interesting works of art. The perfect spot to spend an afternoon reading!

She made a mental note of its location. *I'm definitely coming back here!*

Her quick tour complete, she headed back to her cabin. *Now what to do about dinner?* Eating with strangers did not sound the least bit appealing.

She impulsively decided to order room service. After a quick glance at the limited menu, she settled on a tossed salad with Balsamic Vinaigrette, Honey Sesame Chicken Wings and the Seared Chicken Breast with sundried tomato pesto. *Won't*

hurt to splurge a little since I only had a salad for
lunch.

When her dinner arrived, she carefully carried the tray out onto the balcony. Dining al fresco with magnificent views of the ocean. What could be better?

By the time she finished eating, it was after 9. She changed into her pajamas and crawled into her very comfy bed. Within minutes, she was sound asleep.

Chapter 5

Sam slowly opened her eyes. It was pitch black and her bed was shaking – *bump-bump-bump*. She lay there for a moment, trying to figure out what was making her bed vibrate. Her foggy brain registered there was no tick-tock of her old wall clock and Duke was not laying on top of her, waiting to take his morning jaunt to the backyard.

Suddenly, it dawned on her that this was the first full day of her great adventure. She was on a cruise! Daylight was burning - time to get up and finish exploring the ship!

She threw back the covers and scrambled out of bed. Minutes later, she was standing in the shower, warm water cascading over her head. The shower was tiny but it did the trick. Afterwards, she pulled on a pair of new denim shorts and bright turquoise button down blouse. She ran a comb through her hair and was ready to head up to the Lido deck for a much needed cup of coffee.

Although it was only 7:30, there were large groups of people crowding around, waiting in long lines to reach the impressive breakfast buffet.

She was in no mood to join the masses but couldn't resist glancing at the offerings as she passed by. There were almost too many choices. Any kind of bread or roll you could possibly imagine followed by fresh fruit, thinly sliced layers of cheese and deli meat. Next in line were mounds of piping hot scrambled eggs, crispy piles of bacon, a huge tray brimming with sausage links, baskets full of buttery toast, stacks of pancakes and waffles followed by a variety of pastries.

She paused for a second as she passed by the cream cheese pastries. They looked so decadent - and *so* fattening. As if that wasn't enough, they had an omelet station – made to order eggs. Too many choices in Sam's opinion. And too many calories.

Instead, she grabbed a bagel and a bowl of sliced fruit. On the way back out, she spied the coffee machines. Her breakfast now complete, she headed out to the open deck and settled into a padded lounge chair overlooking the vast ocean. She closed her eyes, took a deep breath and slowly exhaled. She leaned back in her comfy chair. Ahhh, serenity.

She thoughtfully chewed on her Cinnamon raisin bagel. Eating alone wasn't *that* bad. *Fresh ocean air must make you extra hungry.* Sam quickly devoured her breakfast and was ready to start her day.

Hopping out of the chair, she made a hasty decision to head up to the sports deck for a brisk walk around the jogging track. If she kept eating like this, she would definitely need to fit in some exercise every day.

The ocean view was inspiring and Sam quickly finished her first lap around the track when she noticed a man sitting on a bench off to the side. As she passed by him, the hair on the back of her neck stood up. He was studying her. Remembering the creep that was stalking her in the hotel the other night, she wasn't about to take any chances. Up ahead was a set of steps leading down to a lower deck and without hesitation, she ran down them, putting as much distance as possible between her and the staring stranger.

It took less than a minute for Sam to decide what to do next. She strode back to her cabin, grabbed one of her books, a pair of sunglasses and hat and headed up the stairs to enjoy the sea air and sunshine. She couldn't wait to start her new book.

As she rounded the corner of the Solarium in search of what she hoped would be a quiet reading spot, she nearly collided with someone coming from the opposite direction.

She took a step back and mumbled an apology. When she looked up, she realized she was face-to-face with the staring stranger from the jogging track.

Up close, he was well over six feet tall – and drop-dead gorgeous. His hair was jet black and wavy. He had a chiseled jaw and the most beautiful blue eyes she'd ever seen. That were now focusing right on her.

Definitely a hottie. Her face turned red. As if reading her thoughts, he leaned back and shoved his hands into his pants pockets. It was obvious he was well aware of his effect on women.

46

Sam absentmindedly chewed on her bottom lip as she tugged on the edge of her blouse.

Noting her obvious discomfort, he took a step back but not far enough to get rid of that same odd sensation from earlier.

A slow grin spread wide across his face. This encounter did not make *him* the least bit nervous. He was actually enjoying it - he was laughing at her!

Sam regained her composure as she crossed her arms and snapped, "Watch where you're going!" This only made the beautiful stranger smile even bigger!

Her eyebrows knit together, her lips tightened into a thin line. "If you're going to keep looking at me with that ridiculous smile on your face, you can at least tell me what your name is!" She blurted out.

Without a moment's hesitation, the blue-eyed dream murmured, "Michel. Michel Lebeau. I smile because the heavens are smiling down on me at this moment. To meet such a beautiful lady on my first day."

47

Oh no! Not only was he gorgeous, he had a sexy French accent! Clutching her bag tighter, Sam took a step back. "OK Michel. Uh...I would love to stand here and chat but I'm running late to meet someone."

Michel's face fell but he quickly recovered. "Perhaps we will cross paths again. If you are free later – before dinner..." His voice trailed off, not sure how she would react to another encounter.

It was too late. He was talking to thin air. Sam had already turned around and walked back in the direction she just came from.

Ahh... if only he could hear the conversation she was now having with herself. *What is wrong with you? A handsome stranger shows an interest in you and you practically bolt.*

With a mental scolding not to be so paranoid, she once again set out to explore the ship and figure out what to do to pass the time until dinner. What she really wanted to do was find a quiet spot and read but she couldn't go back to the Solarium now and chance another run in.

Chapter 6

Hours later, Sam stood in front of the mirror, dressed for dinner. She was having another one of those I-can't-believe-you're-doing-this-conversations with herself. *Why on earth did I let the maître d' talk me into eating with a bunch of strangers?* Her shoulders hunched over in a sign of defeat. She grabbed her sweater and slowly shuffled to the door. Looking at her, one would have thought she was heading to some unimaginable torture.

Thankfully, all her fears were unfounded and Sam ended up having a wonderful evening. She thoroughly enjoyed all of her dinner companions. Well *almost* all of them.

First, there was Jimmy and Vivian, a thirty-something couple from Southern California with two young children they left at home. They loved to talk and it didn't take long to find out they were on the cruise, celebrating their five-year wedding anniversary.

Next were Beth and Emily, a mother and daughter from Orlando, Florida. They were also celebrating. Emily had just graduated from nursing school.

Last but not least was Lee. He was on the cruise by himself. There was no wedding ring so Sam assumed he was single. Of course, you never could tell these days – there were so many cheaters out there . . . she immediately thought of Anthony.

Lee was the most interesting one at the table and the one who spoke the least. Sam found him extremely attractive with his short blonde hair and piercing green eyes. Even though he was sitting down, Sam could tell he was quite tall.

He was wearing a collared polo shirt with a tattoo peeking out from under the edge of his right sleeve. She couldn't quite make out the shape and didn't want to make it obvious that she was trying to see it. Bulging muscles were accentuated by his dark toned and tanned arms. He didn't look like the type to work outside. Whatever he did, he obviously worked at keeping himself in very good shape!

Admittedly, she was curious as to why such an incredibly good-looking man would be on a cruise by himself.

The dinner started out uneventfully once everyone was seated – well, Sam *thought* it was everyone. Her first clue should have been the two empty chairs.

The waiters, Sutali and Alberto, quickly brought everyone's drink order. Sutali glanced around the table. "Will Miss Gabby and Miss Julia be joining us tonight?"

The group started shaking their heads. With that answer, Alberto shrugged his shoulders and began taking dinner orders.

"WHOA!" "WAIT a minute! Y'all can't eat without **us**!" Everyone at the table looked up. Shimmying towards them was a sight to behold. Gaudy was the first word that popped into Sam's head. A slightly roundish bundle of a woman, squeezed into a teensy-weensy neon lime green Spandex dress was heading towards them.

The woman couldn't have been more than 5 feet tall but the 6" silver glitter Stiletto heels gave her a little boost. She was trying to move quickly but those heels were not cooperating and her ankles wobbled precariously with every step she took.

When she finally reached the table, an up-close encounter revealed flaming red hair and a mass of curls that seemed to shoot out in every direction possible.

By now, Sam was able to get a good look at her outlandish outfit. The tight, skimpy dress was accentuated by a deep V-neck and short, short hemline. She had on more make-up than Sam would ever dare to wear. Her bright red lipstick was almost the same color as her hair.

Sutali pulled out her chair and motioned for her to sit. "Glad you could make it, Miss Gabby."

He pulled out the chair next to her. "Nice to see you, too, Miss Julia."

With Gabby's overpowering presence, it was easy to overlook her companion, a plump brunette wearing bookish glasses. She was dressed a whole lot more conservatively in a printed skirt, pink top and white sweater.

Gabby could take a few pointers from Julia, Sam mused.

Gabby sat down right next to Lee and immediately began flirting up a storm. "Well, aren't you a sight for sore eyes!"

Lee grinned from ear-to-ear. It was the first time Sam had seen him smile!

That was all the encouragement Gabby needed. As she leaned forward to say something to him in a low voice, her voluptuous chest spilled out of the dress and came to rest on the dinner table.

Lee didn't bat an eye – he didn't seem to mind in the least. In fact, he seemed to spend more time talking to her than he did the rest of the group.

Sam snorted in disgust. *Guess you gotta dress like a floozy to get that guy's attention.*

Gabby pretty much monopolized the entire dinner conversation. She was obviously used to being the center of attention. It was extremely annoying and whenever possible, Sam tried to tune her out.

Suddenly, Gabby pushed her chair away from the table and stood up. She grabbed a spoon and started tapping her water glass. "Attention! Attention everyone!"

She continued. "I'm singing Karaoke later this week in the lounge. I'm actually one of the finalists and the winner gets 200 bucks plus 25% off a future cruise."

With one hand on her hip and the spoon still in her other hand, she looked around the table. "You all have to show up and cheer me on!"

Sam leaned back in her chair as she raised her eyebrows and glanced over at Julia. "I wouldn't miss it for the world."

She looked back at Gabby innocently. "What are you going to sing?"

Gabby turned to focus her attention on Sam. "I'm not sure," she admitted. "But I'm thinking maybe Pat Beamatar." She paused before continuing. "People say I sound just like her." After giving everyone the details, Gabby sat back down and turned her attention back to Lee.

Sutali returned to the table and took everyone's dessert order. Sam was more than a little relieved dinner was almost over.

When the coffee arrived, Gabby finally dragged her eyes away from Lee as she looked around the table at the rest of the group.

A broad smile crossed Sam's face. One of big mouth's very long, very fake eyelashes had started to come off and was now dangling precariously in front of her left eye. She started blinking rapidly. The more she blinked, the looser it became.

The artificial appendage suddenly fell off and dropped into her cup of coffee.

Sam sucked in her breath and began giggling. *Do NOT laugh!* She commanded herself. She quickly glanced around, wondering if anyone else had noticed.

Just then, Sutali arrived with their desserts. When he got to Gabby, he gave her an odd look but said nothing. She was still babbling on a mile a minute, completely unaware of the loss.

Sam looked down at Gabby's coffee cup. She was torn. *I really should say something.*

Just when she opened her mouth to speak, Gabby lifted the cup to her lips and took a sip.

Sam's eyes grew wide. She tugged on a stray strand of hair and watched as Gabby set the cup back down on the table.

The fake lash apparently had a little sticky stuff left on it because it was now attached to her upper lip. She looked like Charlie Chaplin with a dose of Lucille Ball.

Amazingly, no one at the table pointed it out right away. They were either outright laughing or had grabbed their dinner napkins and covered their mouths.

Julia, who was sitting next to Gabby, was the last to notice as she finally turned and saw the 'stache. Without saying a word, she reached down and pulled a mirror from her little purse, opened it up and handed it to Gabby.

"What am I supposed to do with this?" Gabby snatched the mirror from Julia's hand as she glanced at her reflection. Her eyes opened wide, her face turned bright red – almost as bright as the color of her hair.

She swiftly peeled her new moustache off and without missing a beat, reached up and re-attached it to her eyelid. To Sam's amazement, she continued talking - as if nothing had happened!

Their excitement for the evening was over and before Gabby could do anything else to further entertain the group, everyone stood up to go.

It was still too early to call it a night so she wandered over to the Monterey Club for a nightcap and hopefully listen to some live music in the lounge. When she got to the entrance, she stopped short. The lounge was half full with mostly couples. The band on stage sounded good and Sam stood there watching several of the couples as they slowly swayed to the romantic melody.

The longer she watched, the more alone she felt. Her eyes welled up with unshed tears. *This isn't helping,* she scolded herself. She abruptly turned on her heel as she wiped her damp eyes with the back of her hand. It was time to call it a night.

Chapter 7

Sam woke with a start. She could hear the Cruise Director, Chris, as he made his morning announcements over the intercom about all the fun-filled activities scheduled for that day. Today's port stop was Mexico. She had planned to take the Mayan City of Tulum tour but completely forgot to book the excursion! Her eyebrows furrowed as she glanced over at the clock on the nightstand. If she hurried, she still might be able to make it!

Thirty minutes later with ticket in hand, Sam dashed down the gangplank and quickly joined the rest of the group. Just in time. The guide was leading the group to the shuttle bus parked nearby.

Sam was at the end of the long line and one of the last to board. Her heart sank as she reached the top step and made instant eye contact with Michel. *Oh no! Now what do I do?*

She glanced around. The bus was almost full and there were only a couple spots left. The first empty seat was next to Michel. The other beside Lee.

She quickly weighed her options and made a beeline for Lee. She could kill two birds with one stone. Avoid Michel and make good on her vow to find out more about the good-looking mystery man that Gabby had monopolized last night.

When she reached the empty seat next to Lee, she paused. "Do you mind if I sit here?"

Lee grudgingly looked up and gave a quick shake of his head.

Sam sighed. *I hope this isn't a mistake.*

It was too late to change her mind now. She settled in next to her reluctant audience of one and started making small talk.

"Have you ever been to Mexico?"

"A few times," Lee answered almost painfully.

Not willing to give up, Sam tried again. "Are you interested in Mayan history?"

"I don't know."

Sam's eyebrows went up. *Well, what on earth was he doing on this tour if he didn't even know if he was interested in the Mayans?*

Before she could ask another question, Lee closed his eyes and leaned his head back on the seat. It was obvious he was in no mood to talk, especially to her!

An hour later, the bus reached the entrance to the Mayan ruins. The only new information she was able to drag out of Lee was that he was an accountant from Ohio. *Hmmm, accountant my foot*, she thought. *His arms look like Popeye's. They must be lifting boxes of copy paper in the accounting office to have them look like that!*

Getting off the bus was slow and tedious and Sam and Lee were the last ones off. The bus was a little worn out and run down and the steps somewhat rickety. Sam hesitantly took her first step. When she got to the second step, her shoe got caught in a small hole. She lost her balance. Her arms flailing, she started to fall forward.

In the blink of an eye, Lee reached around and grabbed her by the waist as he pulled her upright. Miscalculating how light she was, he easily lifted her off her feet and into his arms, leaving the errant shoe wedged tightly in the step.

Lee's strong, muscular arms were firmly wrapped around Sam's petite waist. They stayed that way for a long moment. Lee looked down. *She smelled so nice. She felt even better.* It had been years since he'd been that close to a woman. He hadn't noticed before how fragile she was. Lee was lost in a swirl of feelings and emotions.

Sam was dealing with her own thoughts. It had been a long time since she'd been in a man's arms. It felt wonderful. She lifted her head and gazed up at Lee.

He suddenly realized he was still holding her very close - too close and enjoying it *way* too much. He abruptly set her down. Sam's cheeks turned a bright pink. She'd enjoyed that moment as much as he had. It was more than a little unsettling.

She quickly reached over as she slipped the shoe back on her foot and made her way down the steps without further mishap.

She turned around to thank Lee but he was gone. He was already halfway down the bumpy foot path leading to the ruins.

Sam watched his retreating back as a small smile slowly spread across her face. He was as affected by her close proximity as she was his.

While Lee was heading in the opposite direction, Michel was heading right towards her. Sam warily watched as he approached. There was just something about him...something she couldn't quite put her finger on - that made her slightly uneasy whenever he was around.

Michel didn't waste any time. "Perhaps I can tag along with you this afternoon?" He was determined to accompany her on the tour.

Sam forced a small smile. *I need to give him a chance.* She pushed away her nagging doubts and nodded, giving her full attention to what Michel was saying.

The tour was everything Sam had hoped. She was particularly interested in Mayan history and a visit to Tulum had always been on her bucket list. Their guide was extremely knowledgeable and the entire tour simply fascinating. The scenery was breathtaking – a step back in time. There were no vendors hawking their wares, no skyscrapers towering above, no stoplights and honking cars or streets to navigate.

The entrance to the ancient city was through one of five stone arches. When Sam crossed over, it was like entering a different world. The guide explained that each Mayan city had a specific purpose. Tulum was no exception. It was the only Mayan city built on a coast which made it an important seaport that traded precious stones - mostly turquoise and jade.

Tulum was only one of handful of Mayan cities protected by a wall. The massive limestone structure surrounded the city on three sides. At over 2,500 feet in length and almost 23 feet thick, historians believed the wall had been constructed to protect the nearly 600 priests and nobility that lived inside.

Not much else was known about the Mayans but some locals believed they were either aliens or the lost tribe of Israel, their guide informed the group.

One of the most prominent structures still remaining was the Castillo, or castle. The Castillo was the largest structure inside the protective walls.

Perched on the edge of a limestone cliff, it offered breathtaking views of the Caribbean coast.

Not far from the Castillo was a set of uneven, steep steps leading down to a pristine beach where you could see people cooling off in the turquoise waters or strolling along the soft, powdery sand beach.

Just north of the Castillo was the "Temple of the Winds." It was rumored to have served as the warning system for approaching hurricanes when strong winds would whistle through the openings in the temple. Sam shivered involuntarily. *I can't imagine being stuck in this place during a hurricane.*

In front of the Castillo was one of the better-preserved buildings, the Temple of the Frescoes. Sam peered inside the temple where she could barely make out a faint mural. It was painted in three separate sections. The mural in the first section, or lowest level, represented the Mayan world of the dead. The middle section depicted the living. The third and highest piece was a painting of what the Mayans believed to be the creator of the universe and the rain gods.

Sam's curiosity in Mayan history was the ending of the Mayan calendar in 2012. Although that date had long passed and the world had not come to an end - not that she ever thought it would. Only God knows when the world will end and when his Son will return to earth. One of her favorite Bible scriptures was Matthew 24: 42 – 44 ESV:

"Therefore, stay awake, for you do not know on what day your Lord is coming. But know this, that if the master of the house had known in what part of the night the thief was coming, he would have stayed awake and would not have let his house be broken into. Therefore you also must be ready, for the Son of Man is coming at an hour you do not expect."

One of the frescoes inside the temple depicted a god astride a four-legged animal that historians believe was a horse. If it was a horse, it meant the Mayans still occupied Tulum in 1518 when the Spanish came ashore and it would have been the first time they had ever seen one.

The other fascinating thing about the Mayans was their disappearance. They seemed to have simply vanished without a clear explanation as to what had happened to them. Some theorized when the Spanish arrived, they brought with them sickness and disease. The Mayans immune systems, unable to fight the diseases, were eventually wiped out.

Various buildings around the site depicted what appeared to be a bird's wings and a tail, a Mayan deity whose job it was to protect the people.

Michel and Sam spent the afternoon wandering around the ruins. He was extremely knowledgeable about a variety of topics and kept her entertained with his funny stories of growing up in both Europe and the U.S. He even shared a little about his family. His parents were extremely wealthy French investors. They owned several homes and split their time between them.

Under all the humor and adventure, Sam sensed an unspeakable sadness in Michel. Maybe his parents were so busy when he was growing up, they didn't have a lot of time for a young boy who needed love and attention, she mused.

The afternoon flew by. Soon, it was time to board the bus for the trip back. Sam hesitated for a moment. Should she sit with Michel or finish the trip sitting next to Lee again? Fortunately, she didn't have to make that decision as Lee was sprawled out in his seat with his eyes closed. He hadn't left enough room for her to sit down.

The last stragglers eventually boarded the bus and made their way to their seats. As the bus driver yanked the door shut and started the engine, there was a sudden commotion outside. A masked man abruptly kicked the bus door wide open and bounded up the steps.

He paused when he reached the top. The man briefly flashed what appeared to be a gun as he spoke directly to the driver. "Estoy buscando a miguel." The driver tightly gripped the steering wheel and slowly nodded that he understood. "Si."

The masked man turned and slowly made his way down the aisle. He carefully studied each passenger as he shifted his gaze from one side of the bus to the other. It was obvious he was looking for someone.

By this time, Lee was sitting up, wide awake and intently watching the man's every move.

When the gunman reached the seat she and Michel were sitting in, he paused for a long moment, his eyes narrowing as he focused directly on Michel. She didn't dare glance over in Michel's direction. Instead, she closed her eyes and whispered a quick prayer. By the time she opened them back up, the gunman had finally moved on.

After he reached the rear of the bus and finished inspecting every single seat and every passenger, he slowly walked back towards the front of the bus. He slowed as he passed by Michel and Sam but he didn't stop. *Thank you God*, Sam thought to herself.

Once again at the front of the bus, the masked man stopped and said a few terse words to the driver. The driver vehemently shook his head as he said no over and over. After another second or two and taking another look around, he stepped off.

The driver was not about to wait for him to change his mind as he quickly slammed the door shut, shoved the bus in gear and stomped on the gas pedal. The bus roared out of the parking lot and onto the main road.

You could have heard a pin drop as everyone tried to process what had just taken place.

"What on earth do you think that was all about?" It was hard to read the expression on Michel's face. She couldn't tell if he was rattled or ticked off.

She glanced over at Lee. His expression was about the same as Michel's.

"I have no idea." Michel quietly replied. "But I'm glad that we're out of there."

Lee got out of his seat and walked to the front of the bus to talk with the driver. He was speaking to him in Spanish and you could tell he was asking a question. The driver just kept shaking his head. It was apparent the driver had no idea who the masked man might be.

On his way back to his seat, Lee glanced over at Sam.

She couldn't resist. "What did he say?"

Lee shrugged his shoulders. "He doesn't have any idea who that person was – only that he was looking for someone named Miguel."

They arrived back at the port without further incident. Sam gathered her belongings and shuffled off the bus, careful not to get tripped up on the steps again.

It didn't take long for Michel to quickly catch up with her. "Can I take you to dinner tonight?" Sam glanced over at Michel, her eyebrows went up as she started to laugh - dinner was included in the cruise.

Michel immediately realized what she thinking. "No, I mean to one of the nice, upscale restaurants – not the main dining room."

Sam stopped in her tracks. There was no real reason to tell him no. "That would be nice," she admitted. "What time?"

Well, at least Lee won't have to worry about me prying into his life at dinner tonight she thought. *Now where did that come from?* She wasn't the **least** bit interested in Lee. She was only trying to be nice – at least that's what she tried to convince herself.

70

Sam turned her attention back to Michel. They arranged to meet outside the Positano Grille at 7:00 p.m.

Michel was right on time. Samantha had spent more time than she cared to admit picking out the dress to wear. She finally settled on one of her favorites. A Sapphire blue cocktail-length dress with tiny pearls adorning the scalloped neckline. She nervously tugged on the hem as she watched Michel approach. She wondered nervously what it would be like to have dinner alone with an attractive man after not having been on a date in years.

Michel noticed her discomfort and quickly put her at ease. "You look stunning!" He leaned over and gave her a gentle kiss on the cheek as he squeezed her hand reassuringly.

Sam turned a light shade of pink, not knowing how to reply. "Thanks. You look pretty good yourself." Michel was also dressed to the nines. He looked very European in a black, double-breasted silk suit that was the perfect cut for his frame. His tie was cobalt blue - the exact color of his eyes.

The dining room was filled with overstuffed, high back chairs. The hostess quickly seated them at a corner table. The tables were covered with fine linen cloths and small candles gave the room a romantic glow. The meal was delicious, the wine paired perfectly to their selections and before she knew it, they were sipping coffee and talking as if they had known each other for years.

The conversation drifted to the events on the bus earlier in the day as they wondered who the masked gunman had been looking for. "I'm just glad it wasn't one of us."

Michel face clouded over as he nodded in agreement. "I feel sorry for whoever it is – if this guy ever finds that person."

After leaving the restaurant, Sam and Michel stepped outdoors and onto the deck. The sun had set hours ago. The cool evening air brushed against Sam's bare arms, causing her to shiver.

They made their way over to the railing. The moon was just coming up and cast a romantic glow across the dark, vast ocean.

Sam shivered again. Michel pulled her close as he wrapped his arm around her shoulders in an attempt to warm her. He looked down. His gaze wandered to her lips and lingered there for a long moment. She stared up at him, wondering what it would feel like to have him kiss her.

"Don't miss out on our spectacular, one-of-a-kind Chocolate Buffet now open in our Grand View café!" The cruise director's booming voice rang out over the loudspeaker directly overhead. Startled, Sam jumped back, breaking free from Michel's embrace. "We better get inside. It's getting chilly out here." The spell was broken.

They slowly made their way back to the main part of the ship. Considering what had nearly taken place just now, Sam thought it would not be wise to let Michel walk her to her cabin. When they reached the atrium, she turned to look up at him. "Thank you for a lovely evening."

Michel reached over and grabbed her hand. He hesitated before raising it to his lips and giving it a gentle kiss. "My pleasure."

As he released her hand, she looked at him questioningly. "Perhaps I'll see you tomorrow, then?"

A small smile played across his lips as he answered. "Absolutely!"

On the way back to her room, Sam passed the dining room where she had eaten with Lee and the others the night before. As luck would have it, dinner was ending and she ran into the entire group as they exited the restaurant. Bringing up the rear was Lee.

The group stood in a tight circle as they made small talk about the day. "We missed you at dinner tonight..." Vivian looked over at Sam questioningly.

Sam glanced at the floor and then looked back up at everyone before she answered. "I had dinner in the Positano Grille with a new friend."

Beth and Emily nodded knowingly. Beth replied, "We saw you with the tall, handsome gentleman from earlier today." Lee frowned and did not say a word.

Well! Thought Sam. *You barely said five words to me today so I have no idea how this could possibly bother you.* Sam was irritated when she realized Lee put a damper on her good mood and he shouldn't have.

She wasn't going to allow him to ruin a nice day and with that she quickly said good-night to the group and stomped off.

Halfway back to her cabin, her mood was greatly improved and she smiled as she thought about how much she enjoyed the ruins and dinner with Michel. Except for the masked man on the bus, the day had been perfect.

She quickly got ready for bed. As she drifted off to sleep, she thought about what a wonderful day it had been ...

Chapter 8

The next day was a full day at sea and uneventful for the most part, which made it perfect in every way. Sam started to read her new book, then kicked back in her lounge chair and managed to take a short nap.

She even had a chance to hang out on the pool deck and listen to the steel drums band. She closed her eyes as she tapped her fingers on the chair. The music and warm air definitely made it feel like a Caribbean vacation.

After a light lunch, she took a break and bought some internet minutes so she could check her email and see if there were any emergencies at the office.

When that was done, she headed to what was now one of her favorite places on the ship – the Solarium. A short time later, she was settled in and completely engrossed in her book. She never heard Michel approach and when he suddenly sat down beside her, Sam nearly jumped out of her skin. He seemed distracted and after only a few minutes, told her he needed to head down to the internet café and take care of some business.

Sam was almost relieved when he left and she was quickly caught up in her book again. It was a picture-perfect day for enjoying the sunshine streaming in through the open roof and the peacefulness of the Solarium – worlds away from the crowds and chaos of the pool area.

Finally, she tore her eyes away from the book and looked over at the clock hanging on the wall. It was getting late. She jumped up and started to gather her belongings when she heard her name announced over the ship's intercom system. "Would Samantha Rite please come down to Guest Services?" *Hmm, wonder what that is all about. Must be important if they're paging me.*

For a minute, her mind flashed back to her rebellious high school days when the principal's office would page her over the intercom for some minor infraction. She grinned at the memory. *I hope I'm not in any trouble!*

She made her way down to guest services and a few minutes later was standing at the counter. "Yes, my name is Samantha Rite. I was just paged to come down here."

The uniformed clerk studied her briefly and then reached into the desk drawer, pulling out a room card. She pushed the card across the counter in Sam's direction. "Is this yours?"

She looked down at the card and shook her head, confused. *This couldn't be her card.* She set her bag on the counter and dug around inside. Finally, she emptied all the contents. The room card was not in there. "I can't find my card."

The clerk closed the drawer and folded her hands. "Someone found it in the library and turned it in," she explained. Sam was at a loss. She hadn't been in the library at all. Not even once. "That is really odd."

Puzzled and relieved, Sam took the key. "Thank you. Please tell whoever turned it in I said thank you."

Still perplexed, Sam made her way back to her cabin. At least someone had been kind enough to turn it in.

As she readied for dinner, she wondered if Lee would be there and if he would be any nicer today than he was yesterday.

She didn't have to wait long to find out. When she got to the table, Lee, Gabby and Julia were already seated. Gabby was engrossed in something Lee was saying to her. Julia was sitting there looking uncomfortable as she stared down at her hands.

Sam sat down and turned to Julia. "Are you Gabby's daughter?"

Julia looked up and smiled but before she could answer, Gabby's head snapped around to glare at Sam. "Of course not! Julia's only a few years younger than me! She's my little sister."

"I'm sorry. I just thought..." Sam trailed off.

Just then, Beth and Emily walked up, closely followed by Jimmy and Vivian. Sam breathed a sigh of relief. *Whew! That was a close call! I surely don't want to incur the wrath of Gabby!"*

Sam really enjoyed talking to Jimmy and Vivian and she was more than a little envious of the two. They seemed so happy together. Always talking about their children back home and how after five years of marriage, they still felt like newlyweds.

Maybe someday she would meet the right one...someone that wasn't a cheater, someone she could trust - that really loved her and wanted to be with her.

Without thinking, she said the first thing that popped into her head. "Jimmy and Vivian, you seem so in love. I hope I meet the right man one day."

She instantly wished more than anything she could take the words back - but it was too late. Sam had opened her mouth and stuck her foot in it!

Emily quickly spoke up. "Now that you mention it, we've been curious. You're so nice and so pretty. We're wondering why you're alone."

For a minute, Sam had the deer-in-the-headlights look. She wasn't a good liar so she briefly told them about Anthony. Then she explained her sister's accident and how she ended up on the cruise by herself. Looks of sympathy crossed their faces. That is *exactly* what Sam had hoped to avoid – having people feel sorry for her and why she tried to steer clear of talking about the whole sordid mess.

She cast an uneasy glance in Lee's direction. His expression was unreadable.

Beth turned to Lee. "Now it's your turn. Why are you on this trip alone? Anyone special at home?"

Sam leaned forward and put her elbows on the table, forgetting all about her own discomfort. She was as curious as everyone else.

His expression was unchanged and his voice unemotional as he answered Beth's question. "I was married. I loved my wife very much. She died a couple years ago." For a moment there was an awkward silence.

Sam's heart sank. "I'm sorry if we brought up painful memories." Lee nodded and that was the end of the conversation.

After dinner was over, everyone got up to go their separate ways. Before they could leave, Gabby quickly blurted out. "Don't forget to come by the Excalibur Lounge to watch me sing Karaoke tonight!" It was a good thing she reminded them. Sam had completely forgotten! She wouldn't miss this for the world.

Sam made her way down to the ship's excursion desk. There was no way she was going to forget to book her adventure this time! Tomorrow's port stop was Belize and she was excited about having a chance to go cave tubing in the rainforest.

The US State Department had recently issued travel advisories for Belize in general. The ship's crew did a good job of keeping everyone informed and they were quickly reassured it was perfectly safe. As long as you didn't stray out of the designated tourist areas, there was no need to worry about crime and the recent incidents of unrest.

Sam picked up her tickets and started back to her cabin to drop them off. As she passed by the Burgundy Lounge, she could hear classical music drifting out into the hallway. It was too tempting to pass by so she impulsively stepped inside and made her way to the counter in the back. She ordered a Diet Coke and when she turned around, Michel was directly behind her. He looked stunning in his three-piece suit – it almost took her breath away. He quickly grabbed one of the open barstools next to her. "I've been looking for you all afternoon."

She smiled warmly as he squeezed her arm. "I had a nice, relaxing day – it just flew by." She continued. "So what have you been up to?"

Michel avoided her gaze as he vaguely replied. "Oh, not much of anything, really." He always seemed so open but it was obvious he wasn't going to give her any details.

Oh well, she thought. *It doesn't really matter. I'm enjoying his company and what he does is his own business.*

The two of them were discussing tomorrow's excursion when suddenly she sensed someone standing behind her. She swiveled around and practically crashed right into Lee. Without an invitation, he plopped down in the seat on the other side of her. "Do you mind if I join you?"

Sam put on her best fake smile. "By all means. The more the merrier."

After making small talk about the gorgeous weather and how much they were looking forward to Belize tomorrow, Lee pointedly turned to Michel. "What did you do with your day today?"

What nerve. That was none of his business, Sam thought indignantly. *He was grilling a person he barely knew.*

Sam quickly came to his defense. "I'm sure he did the same things as everyone else. Hung out by the pool. Ate too much. Took a nap ..." she trailed off.

Lee didn't wait for an answer before he turned back to Sam. "So what are your plans for tomorrow? Not another ruins tour, I hope."

"I was tempted to take the Altun Ha tour." She admitted. "But friends of mine who've been to Belize raved on the cave tubing excursion so I decided on that instead."

Sam was surprised when Michel quickly added, "I'm taking that tour, too."

Lee leaned back in his seat, eyebrows raised. "Believe it or not, I'm going cave tubing, as well." He smiled. "Looks like we'll all be on the same excursion again." Whether he was genuinely happy or not – she couldn't tell.

It seemed more than a little odd to Sam that all three of them were once again going on the same excursion...

She didn't have time to dwell on it as she glanced down at her watch. "Better head over to Excalibur. We promised to watch Gabby sing," she reminded Lee.

Without waiting for an answer, Sam turned to Michel. "Care to join us? One of the ladies at our dinner table is singing Karaoke and we agreed to lend some moral support."

When they got to the lounge, they found the rest of the group already sitting at a large table near the front. Lee absentmindedly introduced Michel to the others as he glanced around the dark room.

They made it just in time and the competition quickly got under way. There were five contestants and each person chose a different style of music. There was quite a variety: country, pop, blues and a couple of the singers were very good. Gabby had some serious competition!

Finally, it was Gabby's turn to take the stage. There was a long pause and then suddenly, Gabby dramatically strutted out from behind the massive purple curtain.

Sam slapped a hand over her mouth to keep from laughing. Gabby had on the craziest outfit! Not only that, she had on the most ridiculous wig! The black mop barely covered the pile of red that was shooting out from almost every direction.

As usual, she had tons of make-up on but at least her fake eyelashes were in the right spot. So far. Her outlandish outfit looked like something you'd find in a Halloween costume store. A sleeveless, way-too-tight Leopard print leotard with a deep V-neck that revealed way more cleavage than needed to be displayed.

Sam unconsciously voiced her concern. "Uh-oh."

Vivian knew exactly what Sam was thinking as she chimed in, "I hope she keeps the girls safe inside that get-up or we'll get more show than we bargained for!"

Instead of wearing pants, she had squeezed into a pair of shimmering black nylon stockings. She finished her costume with a pair of 6" high black leather boots.

Gabby paraded onto stage, smiling widely as she walked. It was obvious she loved being the center of attention. She grabbed the microphone and headed to the front.

The first few notes were right on key as she started singing *Heartbroken.* Sam wasn't sure if she was surprised or not. Gabby had a great voice. She sounded *a lot* like Pat Beamatar.

There were a couple tense moments during her performance where she was jiggling around and Sam was wondering if the show was going to become R-rated but thankfully Gabby "held it all together."

When she finished, she got a standing ovation. She deserved it! She definitely knocked it out of the ballpark.

The last two contestants finished their performance. Sam had never heard either of the songs and couldn't tell what genre they were going for. One of them kind of sounded like Frank Sonata. Someone from her parent's era.

The contest was quickly narrowed down to Gabby, the girl singing pop and a rhinestone-studded cowboy singing country. Voting by applause, Gabby narrowly won. When they announced her as the winner, she was ecstatic, jumping around, waving her winnings.

Afterwards, she floated over. Her head held high, eyes gleaming. "I won! I won!" Everyone congratulated her.

In a magnanimous gesture, she flagged down the bartender and ordered a round of drinks on her. After hanging out for half an hour or so, Sam stood up. It was past her bedtime.

Michel stood up, too. Both said their goodnights. When they got to the club entrance, Michel stopped Sam. "Can I walk you back to your cabin?"

The idea made Sam the teensiest bit nervous. She swallowed hard and gave Michel a small smile. "Of course."

When they reached her cabin, they stopped outside the door. By now Sam was getting more than just a little nervous. She stated the obvious. "This is it."

As she turned to say goodnight, he slowly drew her into his arms and gently bent down as he softly kissed her. Sam surprised herself by linking her arms around Michel's neck. She pressed her lips more firmly to his, demanding a more intimate exchange.

Sudden laughter a few doors down brought them quickly back to reality and they guiltily separated. Sam's face turned three shades of red. She looked down, embarrassed that she completely lost control of her senses, even if it was only for a minute.

Michel huskily chuckled, slightly amused by her reaction. "You turn a very pretty shade of pink."

Not wanting to further her embarrassment, he lifted her hand to his lips and gave it a gentle kiss. "I look forward to seeing you in the morning." Without waiting for a reply, he turned on his heel and walked off.

Sam almost ran inside her cabin. She quickly closed the door and bolted it shut. As if he was going to try to break it down! She leaned against the door, chiding herself for acting like a schoolgirl who had never been kissed!

She took a deep breath and stepped out onto her balcony to clear her head. The moon was full tonight. It cast a warm glow over the water. *How romantic. If only I had someone to share it with.*

Afterwards, she lay in bed for hours, tossing and turning, unable to sleep. It wasn't Michel's kiss that was keeping her awake. For some reason, the excursion the next day had her on edge.

For as long as she could remember Sam would - at times - suddenly get an uncanny sense of foreboding. Now was one of them and the feeling grew as she thought about the masked man from the other day.

She finally fell into a fitful sleep, dreaming of masked men chasing her through the jungle. Minutes later her alarm went off. It was time to get up.

Chapter 9

The final port day arrived with bright sunshine and warm tropical breezes. Sam tried to muster some enthusiasm but she was bone-tired.

She showered, slipped on her bathing suit, an old pair of shorts and a ratty, worn t-shirt. She pulled her long hair back into a pony tail. *No sense in dressing nice if I'm going to be trudging through the jungle,* she wisely decided.

The strong sense of foreboding returned without warning. She shook her head, as if to shake it off but knew that wouldn't make any difference. It was here to stay.

Belize was a tender port – the ship was too large to dock at the pier so passengers had to board smaller shuttle boats to take them ashore. There were good-sized waves making the seas a little rough and the twenty-minute ride was somewhat nauseating. *I'm glad I don't get motion sickness.* Being claustrophobic was bad enough!

The shuttle finally docked, Sam made her way off the small boat. She didn't see Michel on the tender and wondered if he would be waiting for her on shore.

The thought of Lee suddenly popped into her head and she was instantly annoyed with the fact that he would be on this excursion. *Well, let's hope he isn't as aggravating today as he was last night.*

Her tour group was waiting at the end of the pier. She quickly realized that not only would Michel and Lee be taking this tour, but Beth and Emily and Jimmy and Vivian would be taking it as well!

"I didn't know you guys were cave tubing today, too. This will be so much fun!" Sam was excited. It would be a great day after all, in spite of Lee and his attitude!

A small bus pulled up to where they were standing on the sidewalk. It didn't take long for them to get on and find a seat. She and Michel boarded at the same time and it was an easy decision for Sam this time as she settled in next to him.

After a quick head count, their guide stepped to the front of the bus as he talked about the tour.

Sam looked around. *Wow! There were only a handful of people taking this tour.* She should have gone with her instinct and skipped the tour but it was too late to change her mind now.

The bus pulled away from the curb. As Sam listened to the guide, she couldn't shake her feeling of uneasiness.

Sam's mind wandered and she missed half of what the guide said to the group. But she did manage to catch the tail end of his speech. "For guests' safety, two armed guards will be accompanying us on this trip."

Sam nervously twisted the ring around her finger as she whispered to Michel. "What did we get ourselves into?" He didn't answer. Instead, he was kicked back in his seat, obviously unconcerned by this new bit of information.

She glanced over at Lee. He was leaning forward, intently watching the guide and both armed guards as they settled in the seats at the front of the bus.

The bus rumbled along until it reached the edge of town a few minutes later. Without warning, the guards pulled a plain brown box from under their seat and quickly emptied it onto the floor. Sam peeked around the edge of the seat to see what it was. There lay a small pile of cheap, multi-colored backpacks.

One of the guards stayed in the front of the bus while the other started towards the back, carrying the backpacks in his arms.

As the guard made his way to the rear, the one in the front started talking. "Place all your belongings including phones, wallets, jewelry, cameras into one of the backpacks we're bringing around." It was a command – not a suggestion and the look on his face told them not to ask any questions.

They all nervously looked around but no one voiced an objection as they emptied their stuff into the bags. When everyone finished filling the bags, they were taken to the front of the bus and put back in the big cardboard box.

Sam's mind was reeling. She couldn't even begin to digest what had just happened. She sent up a quick, fervent prayer for God's protection which made her feel somewhat better. Michel reached over to squeeze her hand reassuringly but said nothing.

The next two hours were spent in uncomfortable silence. No one dared speak. For Sam, it was the fear of hearing something she didn't want to.

They drove along at a fast pace for a good ten miles, Suddenly, the bus abruptly veered off onto a bumpy dirt road causing Sam to almost fall out of her seat.

This got everyone's attention as they all focused on the driver and the front of the bus. He was clearly nervous and kept glancing into the mirror. When one of the guards noticed him looking back, he positioned himself so that the driver was no longer in view.

The hair on the back of Sam's neck stood up. Something was not right. The group started whispering to each other in low voices.

It was easy to see they were heading deep into the jungle as they rattled along the deserted, dirt road. With each passing mile, Sam became more and more frightened. Something was very, very wrong.

She quickly glanced at Michel. His face was expressionless.

She swallowed hard and then whispered. "This does not look good." He shook his head in response. Gone was his look of nonchalance from earlier.

Lee suddenly stood up and started walking to the front of the bus. A guard quickly turned to face him. "Return to your seat!" he commanded.

Lee paused for a moment and then turn around as he headed back to his seat. After all, he wasn't the one with the gun.

Finally, after what seemed like an eternity, the bus came to a screeching halt. A dust cloud swirled around the bus. The air was so thick, Sam could no longer peer out the windows.

When the dust settled, the "guards," the tour guide and the bus driver all stood up at the same time. One of the guards yanked the door open and quickly made his way down the steps. The instant his foot touched the ground, five masked and armed strangers in camouflage suddenly appeared from out of the thick jungle.

The bus erupted into mass confusion. Someone yelled, "Get down. Get under the seats." Others started crying. The entire scene seemed so surreal. Sam's mind could not register what was taking place.

Michel sat quietly, watching the scene unfolding. He reached over to put a protective arm around her shoulder.

Sam glanced over at Lee. The look on his face appeared calm but his eyes were narrowed and he was intently watching the activity taking place outside.

The guard left standing at the front of the bus started yelling. "Everyone off!"

The driver moved a step closer to the lone gunman onboard. "What's going on here?" he demanded.

It was the wrong thing to say. The guard turned his gun on the driver. "You get off first." The bus driver nervously glanced at the passengers in the back. He looked back at the gunman as he wiped his brow and made his way down the stairs.

He had almost reached the bottom when the guard lifted the gun and pointed it at the back of his retreating head. Without warning, he pulled the trigger. The driver tumbled forward, ending up face down in the dirt, blood pouring from the wound. He lay there motionless, leaving little doubt in anyone's mind that he was dead.

Chaos ensued. Everyone on the bus started screaming and yelling.

The guard who seconds before had killed the driver, turned his attention back to the passengers and pointed his gun at them. "Silence!" The bus was instantly quiet. Sam could almost smell the fear in the damp air of the small bus.

A loud buzzing noise filled her head. "I'm going to faint." She dropped into her seat. The eerie silence lasted for several long seconds as she tried to control her breathing and get rid of the dizziness that was trying to take over.

Michel carefully stepped over Sam and walked to the front of the bus. "Who's in charge here?" For a moment the guard studied Michel. Sam turned her attention to where Michel was now standing, certain he would be shot next.

He motioned Michel off the bus. "Follow me." With that, he led Michel towards the armed group waiting outside. Sam's heart sank. Michel was next! They were going to shoot Michel!

There was nothing to do but watch the scene unfold. Michel began speaking to them in fluent Spanish.

Sam held her breath as they all stared at Michel. *I sure wish I knew what was being said!*

After a few tense moments, one of the guards roughly grabbed Michel's arms and forced them behind his back. The armed bandit pulled a pair of handcuffs from his pocket and swiftly clamped them on Michel's wrist. Michel put up a brief struggle but it was futile. The gunman pointed his weapon at Michel's head and he immediately stopped fighting.

When they finished putting the cuffs on, they blindfolded him. Three of the armed intruders dragged him off into the jungle and out of sight.

Sam closed her eyes and started praying fervently. *Dear God. Please protect us.*

Psalm 91:15 popped into Sam's head: ***"... He shall call upon me, and I will answer him: I will be with him in trouble; I will deliver him, ..."*** *(KJV)*

She prayed for Michel and all the other passengers on board. She prayed for the poor bus driver who was shot in cold blood right before her very eyes.

This isn't happening, she kept repeating to herself. *It's just a bad dream.*

"Everyone off the bus!" The guard yelled. "NOW!" Sam's eyes flew open. Not a peep or murmur was heard as everyone quickly shuffled off. They tip-toed past the poor bus driver who was still lying on the ground in a pool of blood.

Just as the last person got off, a large box truck pulled in behind the bus. The driver quickly jumped out, walked to the back and flung the door open. "Everyone in!"

The frightened passengers had no more scrambled into the back of the dirty, cramped truck when the driver yanked the door shut and shoved the lock in place. Soon the truck started off down the same dirt road, heading even deeper into the jungle.

Chapter 10

Sam quickly realized there were no armed guards in the back of the truck with them. People began praying, some started crying while others tried to formulate an escape plan. It seemed hopeless.

Although it was dark inside the box, Sam could faintly make out Lee's outline. He seemed to be very focused on something he had in his hand. *Maybe he has a phone or some way to communicate what was happening and that they were in trouble!*

Lee must have sensed Sam's stare. He looked up at her with an expression of warning that told her not to say anything. She slowly nodded her head that she understood.

Sam felt a glimmer of hope. Maybe there was a chance someone would find out what was happening and they would be rescued!!

Sam prayed again. *Please God. Help us find a way out safely.* She ended with another quick prayer for Michel, even though he was probably already dead.

As the truck rumbled along, Sam's claustrophobia kicked into high gear. Her heart started pounding rapidly and she panicked as she gulped the stale, musty air.

She closed her eyes and leaned her head back as she tried to take her mind off the stifling heat. It felt like a tomb. A very hot tomb.

After what seemed like hours, the truck abruptly stopped. The back door flew open. For a moment, the bright sunlight was blinding as it filled the back of the truck. Sam blinked, trying to focus her eyes. Thank God they were getting out!

The driver eventually came into focus. "Everyone out," he demanded.

Sam and the others crawled out of the back and looked around. They were in some sort of a makeshift camp in the middle of the jungle. Several tents dotted the site. There was a campfire burning. Rickety old Army cots were scattered about and a bunch of blue plastic coolers were piled up in a small covered shelter off to the side. This abduction had been carefully planned!

The group was settled into small rows under the watchful eyes of the guards. Sam furtively studied her abductors. Even though all of them wore masks, one of them was much smaller than the others and Sam was sure it was a female.

Chaotic thoughts tumbled around in her head. *Why them? What was the purpose of hijacking an entire bus full of tourists and bringing them to this remote jungle? They had all their belongings – everything of value. What more could they possibly they want?*

The afternoon crept slowly by as the group restlessly swatted at mosquitos and tried to avoid other creepy-crawly critters scurrying around the camp. The heat was almost unbearable. Sweat poured down Sam's face. Her hair was plastered to her face and neck, her clothes soaking wet.

Dusk was settling in and the weary group was not only drenched in sweat, they were hungry and thirsty. As the hours wore on, the group grew more and more restless. It was obvious they needed food and water.

Finally, Beth bravely spoke up. "Can't you see that we're all hungry and thirsty?" The one that appeared to be the leader of the small group walked over to Beth. He stood there as he studied her for a moment. Beth swallowed hard but refused to look away as she stared down her abductor.

After what seemed like an eternity, he abruptly turned on his heel and made his way over to the coolers in the makeshift tent. Without saying a word, he returned moments later with bottles of ice cold water and brown paper bags.

He made his way down the line, handing a bottle of water and paper bag to each person. Grateful for whatever they were given, the group quickly gulped down the water.

After finishing off all her water, Sam slowly unfolded the paper bag and cautiously peered inside. Her heart sank. It was a peanut butter & jelly sandwich and a banana. Despite the unappealing food, there was no way she was going to complain. She quickly ate the soggy sandwich and over-ripe brown banana.

She crumpled up her bag and looked around. Lee was staring in her direction. His eyes tried to reassure her that everything would be OK. Sam attempted a small smile but quickly gave up. She was absolutely terrified and there was no way anything short of a miraculous rescue would make her feel better.

After everyone finished eating, they were separated into small groups. The person Sam now believed was the leader began barking orders on who would be sleeping in what tent.

Sam was assigned the same tent as Jimmy and Vivian. Beth and Emily were put in the same tent as Lee. She was thankful mom and daughter hadn't been separated but disappointed that she wasn't with Lee. She wanted to find out what he had been doing earlier and if it could offer any glimmer of hope for a rescue.

Sam ducked inside the tent and cautiously crawled into one of the sleeping bags. She squeezed her eyes shut but falling asleep was not going to happen. She was convinced that if she fell asleep, something creepy and hairy with lots of little legs and hundreds of beady little eyes would most certainly make its way into her sleeping bag and it probably wouldn't be wise if she started screaming.

She lay motionless in the hot, stuffy tent for what seemed like endless hours. As she stared up at the top of the tent, all the terrifying events of the day raced through her mind like a b-rated, scary movie that refused to end.

Without warning, there was a loud commotion on the other side of the camp. Seconds later, their tent door was ripped open. A long arm reached in and grabbed Jimmy by the feet, pulling him roughly through the opening. Vivian started to scramble to the outer edge of the tent, away from the door. Before she could reach the other side, another dark, sinister figure rushed in, grabbing her by the arm and half dragging, half carrying her from the tent. She opened her mouth to scream but was quickly silenced as a strong hand clamped over her face.

Sam could hear Jimmy's muffled voice nearby. "Please! Don't hurt my wife," Jimmy begged.

After several long, agonizing moments, it grew eerily silent.

By now, the rest of the group inside the tent were sitting upright. Too shocked to do anything, they stared blankly at the empty sleeping bags Jimmy and Vivian had just been occupying. Samantha shuddered uncontrollably as she prayed that God would protect them from harm.

The nightmare they were in was getting worse by the minute. First Michel and now Jimmy and Vivian. Is this how they would all die? Being dragged out one at a time to who knows what kind of torture and torment? *I'm going to lose it,* Sam thought.

Her mind wandered to Brianna. Would she know how much her mom loved her – that she'd been thinking of her in what could be the last hours of her life?

Sam's stomach grew queasy and she started to feel physically ill. She swallowed hard, trying to push down the nausea that threatened to overtake her.

She pushed aside the thought of never seeing her beautiful daughter again and focused on getting out of there alive. She needed to find out what Lee was thinking – what chance of rescue he thought they might have. And fast! They were running out of time...

She forced herself to calm down. *Breathe in, Breathe out, Breathe......*

"Nooooooo!!!!!!!!" More screaming broke the eerie calm. And it was right outside their tent.

Sam burrowed down into her sleeping bag, sure that this was the end of them all. She lay there motionless. Terrified as the noises grew louder and even closer. She could hear the muffled sounds of men shouting and screaming. It sounded like hundreds of people pounding the ground outside.

Pop! Pop! Pop! Several gunshots rang out mere feet from the tent.

In an instant, it went from deafening sound to complete silence. The commotion ended as quickly as it began.

Sam slowly pulled the blanket off her head. She held her breath and listened intently. Nothing but eerie silence. There was no movement. There was no yelling. There were no more gunshots.

The only thing Sam could hear now was her own pounding heart. *Surely I'm about to have a heart attack*, she thought.

A faint shadow crept over her. Someone had entered the tent and now stood hovering over the top of her. She squeezed her eyes tightly shut. Every instinct told her to play dead. Maybe whoever it was would think she had been shot.

Sam felt a sharp tug on the edge of her sleeping bag. Her whole body numb with fear. She was about to meet her maker. Death was imminent. She put both hands over her face, covering her eyes. She didn't want to see her killer.

"Sam." She heard a voice softly say her name. A familiar voice.

"*Sam*," more insistently this time. Her eyes flew open. In the darkness, she could only see the outline of a face but she knew that voice – it was Lee! He had something in his hand. With a flick of the switch, light filled the interior of the small tent. Lee was looking down at her, flashlight in hand.

She was quite a sight. Her green eyes were wide with fear. Her hair was no longer pulled back in a tidy pony tail. It looked like she had stuck her head in a wind tunnel and then rolled around in a pile of twigs and debris. Her makeup was smeared and tear-stained mascara lines ran down her face.

Dazed, she sat up and looked at Lee. The others in the tent sat up and were staring at Lee, too.

He gazed around at the small, terrified group. "You're safe. You're all safe." He was talking but his words weren't registering ....

The wary captives slowly emerged from their sleeping bags and made their way out into the cool evening air.

The camp was in shambles. Some of the abductors lay dead on the ground. The ones that were still alive huddled in a small group, surrounded by armed men in military garb.

In the distance, loud engines could be heard. The rumbling grew louder and louder as it got closer and closer. Soon, the dense foliage parted as all-terrain military vehicles pushed through the thick trees and overgrown brush. Within minutes, the entire area was surrounded. Sam wanted to drop to her knees and kiss the ground in relief.

As she stood there taking it all in, she spotted Lee out of the corner of her eye, talking to one of the men. The man was wearing a military uniform and looked to be the person in charge.

Lee's brows were bunched together, his mouth set in a hard line as he leaned in to say something to the other man. From the expressions on their faces, they were having a very intense conversation. She wondered if it had anything to do with Michel or Jimmy and Vivian.

At the thought of her three friends, Sam was filled with sadness and consumed by guilt. She was safe and they were all probably dead by now.

Poor Michel. He had been trying to help. God only knows what kind of torture he went through at the hands of this ruthless bunch. She also thought about the poor bus driver. Hopefully they would be able to find his body and give him a decent burial.

Jimmy and Vivian were so full of life. What would become of their children? How could you explain to the families that merciless criminals had cold-heartedly killed their loved ones?

Sam's eyes filled with tears as she tried to push back a sea of emotions that threatened to overtake her. There would be plenty of time to relive the horrifying ordeal later.

They stood around for a few more minutes before being ushered into the waiting vehicles. The long ride back to civilization was eerily quiet. The shock of all they had gone through and the fact they were really safe hadn't sunk in yet.

Eventually, the vehicles pulled up in front of a quaint hotel in downtown Belize City. One by one, the weary passengers crawled out of the vehicle and filed into the hotel. They must have been quite a sight.

The hotel staff gazed at the disheveled, stinky, dirty little group sympathetically. They quickly rushed forward to pass out room keys and more bottles of ice cold water. Sam gratefully accepted the water and the key.

Before being dismissed, they were instructed to return to the front lobby in two hours for a brief meeting.

Sam made her way to her room. She opened the door and flipped on the light switch. It wasn't very large but had everything she would need. The first thing on her agenda was to take a nice, cool shower!

The shower felt wonderful. She scrubbed hard, trying to get rid of not only the dirt and grime covering her body but to remove the terrifying scenes that would not stop running through her head.

She glanced over at the dirty pile of clothes lying on the floor. She had nothing else to change into. The thought of putting the stinky clothes back on didn't make her happy but at least she would smell a little better.

The time flew by and soon all of them had gathered in the main lobby. They were then led in to a small conference room in the rear of the hotel.

In the back of the room, a large table full of food lined one wall. It all looked so delicious! There were piles of deli sandwiches, a huge bowl of pasta and potato salad, tortilla chips and salsa, a bowl of fresh fruit, deserts of every kind and most importantly, bottled water.

Sam couldn't seem to drink enough water. She twisted the lid off and quick downed the entire contents in less than a minute. Eyeing the food, it dawned on her that she was absolutely famished. She grabbed a paper plate nearby and piled her plate high with a little bit of everything. It all tasted wonderful but her favorite was the chips and salsa. The Mexican salsa was fresh and spicy. Sam frowned just before popping a final salsa-laden chip into her mouth. *This will probably come back to haunt me later.*

Sam glanced around the room. Lee was there and had changed into jeans and a t-shirt. He was talking to the same uniformed guy that was in the jungle. It was obvious they knew each other. Sam wondered about Lee's role. Was he some kind of undercover agent? That would explain his secretiveness and why he never offered too much information about himself.

Did he know an abduction had been planned? Was that why he was on the cruise? On that excursion? It was obvious Lee was more than just a casual tourist.

Before she could dwell on it any longer, the officer in charge asked everyone to be seated. Without going into great detail, Lieutenant Commander Ballard (who finally offered his name and title), explained that the military had learned that an abduction had been planned for their cave tubing excursion.   The US Government was very interested in capturing as many of the abductors alive as possible, especially the ringleader, so a strategic trap had been set to flush out the bad guys.

He assured them they were never in any real danger as the captors had specific targets.

"What about Michel and Jimmy and Vivian?" someone asked.

"We did a search of the site and there was no trace of any of them," the Lieutenant admitted. "But we'll begin an extensive search tomorrow."

"How can you be so sure we weren't in any imminent danger? If we weren't in any real danger, why was the bus driver was killed?" someone else asked.

"Unfortunately, the bus driver was one of the bad guys. They found out he was double-crossing them so they killed him," he replied.

"Answering the question on why we were so confident you were all safe..." Lieutenant Commander Ballard turned and pointed at Lee. "You were protected by one of the finest Navy Seals in US history."

Navy Seal? You could have knocked Sam over with a feather! Sam was stunned. The Lieutenant continued speaking but she barely heard the rest of what he had to say.

She managed to catch the tail end of his speech when he told the group that their cruise ship had left port the day before. "Your luggage and all your belongings were removed from the ship and are on their way here now. Each of you should have your bags within the hour."

There were sighs of relief all around the room. Hooray for clean clothes! That was awesome news!

Sam looked down at her filthy rags. *These are going right in the trash!*

He continued. "We made flight arrangements for all of you. Plane tickets will be delivered to your room, along with your luggage."

"Taxis will be waiting out front in the morning to take you to the airport."

It was obvious that the meeting was over.

Without waiting for an invitation, Sam walked straight over to where Lee was standing. She had questions that deserved answers and she was not going to take "no" for an answer.

But it was too late! By the time she got there, Lieutenant Commander Ballard was once again talking to him. Lee saw her out of the corner of his eye and motioned for her to wait a minute.

She retreated to the back of the room, arms crossed as she tapped her foot on the ground. Relief and anger were wreaking havoc on Sam's emotions.

On the one hand, she was ticked off that she had feared for her life while he knew all along what was happening. But on the other, she was relieved they were all safe – except for Michel, and Jimmy and Vivian.

Sam stood there cooling her heels for a few more minutes before Lee finally made his way over to her. She opened her mouth to speak but Lee put up his hand to stop her. "I have some loose ends to wrap up. Can I meet you for dinner in a couple hours?"

He searched her face, waiting for an answer. "I'll try to answer some of your questions then," he added.

She paused for a minute and then nodded her head. She really didn't have a choice. "OK, I guess I can wait." It would give her some time to mull over the questions she had and make sure she wasn't missing anything.

Chapter 11

When she got back to her room, Sam's luggage was already there. Not only that, the backpack with all the stuff she reluctantly handed over to the abductors was there. She'd almost forgotten about it!

She opened the backpack first and reached inside. Yes, her cell phone was in there! She set her rings and watch on the nightstand and then reached for her suitcase. Clothes...Clean clothes were inside!! She rummaged through the rest of her bags. Nothing appeared to be missing.

On her way to the bathroom, she noticed a white envelope lying on the desk. She opened the envelope and pull out a set of plane tickets with her name on it. Her flight was scheduled to leave around 9:30 in the morning. *Better set my alarm this time.*

Inside the bathroom, it didn't take long for Sam to pull off her dirty, old clothes and make good on her vow to throw them out. She took another long, luxurious shower and then slipped on her favorite new summer dress – one she hadn't had a chance to wear yet.

It had been a long, horrifying ordeal and the weight of all that happened was finally setting in. Sam walked over to the mirror and critically studied her reflection. *Damaged goods, that's what I am.*

Nothing but false advertising. The cancer was gone but the scars were a constant reminder. Maybe that's why Anthony left. He couldn't stand to look at her repulsive body any longer.

The stress of the last few days had brought all kinds of buried thoughts to the surface. Thoughts that for years she carefully kept tucked away in the dark recesses of her mind.

She was deeply flawed. Even if she fell in love, how would she go about telling someone about "that?"

Do you casually mention it over dessert – *oh, by the way....*

Maybe when you're laying out by the pool you start off by saying, *"Just thought I should mention ...."*

Or do you let him find out on his own, when there's no turning back?

A sad face gazed back at her in the mirror. No answer would be given. She turned and slowly walked out the door.

Chapter 12

Lee was already waiting for her when she got to the hotel lobby. She was surprised to see him dressed in uniform. She was staring at a complete stranger. An extremely handsome stranger at that!

She made her way over to where he was waiting. He smiled down at her. A warm, wonderful, genuine smile. He looked so different when he wasn't scowling!

"I hope you like the restaurant I picked out for us. There are a couple here at the hotel but this one is my favorite and it has a great view," he explained. Apparently he'd been here before.

He led her outside into the courtyard. The sun had just gone down and dusk settled over the city. Tiki torches cast a romantic glow as they lit the cobblestone path leading to the intimate restaurant.

At the hostess station, Lee gave the girl working there a charming smile. "Can you put us somewhere in a quiet corner – preferably with a nice view?"

She smiled back at him, batting her eyes. "Yes, of course. I have the perfect spot!" She grabbed a couple menus and then led them to a corner table. The table for two was covered with a white linen cloth and small votive candle cast a warm glow. It was just right – very intimate with lush tropical plants everywhere. There was even a small, bubbling fountain nearby.

Sam dismissed the little flirt with a nod of her head. "This will do. Thank you," she coldly added.

Lee pulled out her chair but not before she caught the surprised look on his face.

Sam sniffed. "That little girl needs to flirt with someone her own age."

Lee was smiling as he sat down across from her, an amused expression on his face.

"Well, it's true!" she insisted. But then she mentally reprimanded herself. *I'm so stressed out, I'm getting worked up over nothing!*

Sam picked up the menu. Everything sounded so good. She finally decided on a small dinner salad and Baked Lobster Ravioli with a side of buttery garlic knots. After hearing what she ordered, Lee agreed that sounded delicious and ordered the same.

The waiter walked off and Sam turned to Lee. "Hmm....where should I start?"

Lee cut her off at the pass as he put up a wary hand. "I'm sure you have a ton of questions. Just remember, I'm only allowed to share certain information," he reminded her. "The investigation is on-going so I'm limited in what I can tell you."

Sam had to admit he was probably right. "I know you can't tell me much but can you tell me if Michel or Jimmy and Vivian were ever found?" She held her breath. The answer might not be what she wanted to hear.

"We've gone over the entire area with a fine tooth comb and haven't found a trace of any of them," he admitted.

Lee started to say something else but abruptly stopped. Sam was about to ask him what he was going to say but thought better of it. The look on his face told her the subject was closed.

Lee went on to tell her everything he could, which wasn't much more than what she already knew.

Dinner arrived and the conversation turned to their own personal lives. They talked about their childhoods, where they grew up, where they lived now. Lee told her his parents were alive and living in Texas. He was a middle child with an older and younger sister.

Sam nodded. "Funny, I'm a middle child, too. But I have an older sister and younger brother."

Sam went on to tell Lee about Bri's plans. "My daughter is pestering me to move south – somewhere warmer." She sighed. "I think she has her sights set on Florida."

Lee laughed. "My hometown is actually Northeast Ohio but I've been living in Georgia for the past ten years. I've been tossing around the idea of moving to Florida but haven't made a final decision on that one yet." This time Sam was sure he was telling her the truth.

There was a pause. Lee stared at Sam for a long moment before he slowly leaned forward and spoke earnestly. "I'm sorry I had to deceive you, Sam.

I felt guilty every time I did. That's why I never said too much. I thought the less I said – the less I would have to lie."

Sam looked at him as she shook her head. "Yeah, I was pretty sure you weren't an accountant..."

Lee reached for her hand and held it in a warm embrace. "Can we start over?"

She smiled back at him, her eyes shining brightly. "Yes – Absolutely!"

Finally, Lee explained he would be staying behind in Belize for a while longer. "I know you're flying out in the morning. Can I get your number and give you a call as soon as I'm back in the States?"

Sam's heart skipped a beat. She secretly hoped he would ask but was afraid to suggest it first. She didn't want to seem like some desperate, lonely woman who jumped from one man to the next, even though she had been attracted to Lee first and he had all but pushed her away.

After exchanging phone numbers, Lee walked Sam to her room. When they reached her room, she turned around to face him. Her head tilted to the side thoughtfully as she softly spoke. "Thank you for saving us. I'm sure we will never know half of what actually took place."

As she turned to put her key in the door, Lee caught her hand and slowly pulled her towards him, his arms circling her waist. Lowering his head, he captured her lips in what started out as a sweet, gentle kiss. Her arms reached up as she wrapped them around his neck and pressed her body to his.

The kiss was light and teasing at first. With lightning speed it deepened, becoming fierce and gentle all at once.

Using a control he thought he no longer possessed, Lee finally pulled away. He drew a sharp breath. "I'm sorry. I don't know what came over me."

Sam's eyelids fluttered open as she looked up at Lee. She wasn't sorry. Sam wasn't the least bit sorry. The kiss left her breathless and lightheaded. And she only wanted more. Those thoughts made her turn a bright shade of pink.

Sam blurted out exactly what she was thinking. "I'm not sorry you kissed me. I'm not sorry one little bit." With that, Sam opened the door and went inside, a small smile lighting her face.

****

Sam closed the door and leaned against it heavily. She was exhausted. The week had been a rollercoaster of emotions – deception, excitement, adventure, terror, a lot of relief and last but not least, a little romance. She shook her head. Her family and friends would never believe it. She barely believed it herself.

Early the next morning, Sam met Beth and Emily in the dining room for breakfast. She sat down across from the girls and grabbed the menu. "I'm ready to go home." Emily nodded in agreement. "We were just saying the exact same thing."

Sam filled them in on Brianna's plans to move somewhere warm and how she was leaning towards moving to Florida. "I think she's planning a trip to the Orlando area soon to check it out."

Beth looked at Sam questioningly. "Didn't you say you were from Michigan?"

When Sam nodded, Beth shook her head. "It's a small world. I grew up in West Michigan. Moved down here years ago, right after high school."

Sam set her coffee cup down. "That's where I'm from! Grand Rapids area!"

"Well, I'll be darned."

The two women compared notes and discovered that not only were they from the same area, Sam's older sister Deb and Beth had gone to high school together.

"I know your sister! We used to be friends!" Beth was shocked.

Sam shook her head in amazement. "Wait 'til I tell Deb!"

Beth grew excited as she thought about Sam and her daughter moving to Florida. She looked over at Emily. "We'd love to take her around, show her how the locals live. We can give her some pointers on good areas of town and where she might be happy moving to."

Sam brightened instantly. Now that was a great idea! "Absolutely. I'd be forever grateful if you

130

could – or would. She knows nothing about the area – except how to find the amusement parks!"

Before leaving the restaurant, they exchanged numbers and promised to stay in touch.

****

Sam didn't see Lee again. She knew he was close by and it gave her an odd sense of comfort. She checked out of the hotel and stepped outside. A taxi was there waiting to take her to the airport.

As the plane taxied down the runway and away from Lee, Sam said a quick prayer for his and the other's safety. She added a small prayer that she would hear from him soon.

Moments later, Belize disappeared below the fluffy white clouds.

The end.

About The Author

Hope Callaghan is an author who loves to write Christian books, especially Christian Mystery and Cozy Mystery books. Born and raised in a small town in West Michigan, she now lives in Florida with her husband.

She is the proud mother of one daughter and a stepdaughter and stepson. When she's not doing the thing she loves best - writing books - she enjoys cooking, traveling and reading books.

Hope loves to connect with her readers!

Visit **hopecallaghan.com** for information on special offers and soon-to-be-released books!

Email: hope@hopecallaghan.com

Facebook page:
http://www.facebook.com/hopecallaghanauthor

Other Books by Author, Hope Callaghan:

DECEPTION CHRISTIAN MYSTERY SERIES:

Waves of Deception: Samantha Rite Series Book 1
Winds of Deception: Samantha Rite Series Book 2
Tides of Deception: Samantha Rite Series Book 3

GARDEN GIRLS CHRISTIAN COZY MYSTERIES SERIES:
Who Murdered Mr. Malone? Garden Girls Mystery Series Book 1
Grandkids Gone Wild: Garden Girls Mystery Series Book 2
Smoky Mountain Mystery: Garden Girls Mystery Series Book 3
Death by Dumplings: Garden Girls Mystery Series Book 4
Eye Spy: Garden Girls Mystery Series Book 5
Magnolia Mansion Mysteries: Garden Girls Mystery Series Book 6
Missing Milt: Garden Girls Mystery Series Book 7
Book 8 Coming Soon!

CRUISE SHIP CHRISTIAN COZY MYSTERIES SERIES:

Starboard Secrets: Cruise Ship Cozy Mysteries Book 1
Portside Peril: Cruise Ship Cozy Mysteries Book 2
Lethal Lobster: Cruise Ship Cozy Mysteries Book 3

Visit my website for new releases and special offers: hopecallaghan.com

Preview of Book 2 (*Winds of Deception*)

Winds of Deception

Samantha Rite Series Book 2

Hope Callaghan

FIRST EDITION

hopecallaghan.com

Copyright © 2014
All rights reserved.

"And the sea gave up the dead which were in it, and death and Hades gave up the dead which were in them; and they were judged, every one of them according to their deeds."

Revelation 20:13. KJV

Chapter 1

Sam's eyebrows scrunched together as she scowled at the phone, as if staring at it hard enough would make it disappear. She was never going to get the Collier quote done if the stupid phone didn't stop ringing! She growled at it in frustration. To say Sam was irritated would be an understatement. The 60 hour work-weeks were wearing on her. Instead of shrinking, the piles just seemed to grow.

She ran a frazzled hand through her long dark hair. All this stress and aggravation was the direct result of her recent vacation. Admittedly, the cruise had been a welcome break but the mountain of work waiting for her when she got back left her wondering whether it was worth taking the time off.

Sam sighed heavily as she picked up the phone. "Thank you for calling Anderson Insurance Group. Samantha Rite speaking. How can I help you?"

"Samantha Rite, this is Special Agent James Donovan of the CIA." He got right to the point. "I need to meet with you as soon as possible."

Sam stared down at the phone in disbelief. "Why on earth do you need to meet with me?"

"We believe your life may be in danger," the caller responded.

This must be some kind of joke and it wasn't one bit funny. She had enough to worry about right now. "Sorry, I didn't catch that last part. Did you just say my life was in danger?"

The caller ignored her question and continued talking. "I'm in town now and close to your office. I can meet you there or someplace else ... if you prefer." He paused for a second before he went on. "We need to meet today. The sooner the better."

He quickly continued before Sam could interrupt again. "Lee Windsor asked me to contact you. He's still in Central America and wasn't able to make it himself. Since this is of utmost urgency, I agreed to come here and meet you instead."

Sam let out a mental sigh of relief. Well, at least Lee wasn't blowing her off. There had only been one short text from him since she got home. Last she knew, he was still in Belize and she was beginning to wonder ....

She snapped back to the conversation at hand. "I'm not meeting you anywhere until you tell me what's going on."

Poor Lee, Donovan thought. *This lady sounded like a real handful. Maybe he just caught her at a bad time....*

Donovan repeated himself as he tried to stress the urgency in meeting, "Like I said before, there's a good chance your life may be in danger."

It looked as if Sam wasn't going to get any more information out of this Donovan fellow until she agreed to meet him. She mentally shrugged. It was probably best to err on the side of caution.

"OK, I'll meet you after I get out of work. There's a pub right around the corner from my office. But I can't make it until around 6," she warned.

As soon as she hung up, she texted Lee. *"I just got a call from a man who said he was Special Agent Donovan. He told me my life was in danger and he mentioned your name. Do you know what this is about?"* Sam set her phone down. Hopefully, he would reply.

She spent the rest of the afternoon trying to focus on work but a thread of concern kept winding its way into her thoughts. *Was she really in danger?*

Her mind wandered back to her recent vacation. She and her sister had planned a girls-only cruise – a 40th birthday celebration with a week spent in paradise. A much-needed escape after a really difficult year.

She let out a small sigh. Sam found out her husband had been cheating on her with a woman in his office – a much younger woman at that. It seemed like everyone in the world knew about it - except her. By the time the whole affair was out in the open, there was no chance of salvaging their marriage. Not that Anthony had tried – or even wanted to. The ink wasn't even dry on the divorce papers before the jerk married the "other woman."

The cruise hadn't exactly turned out as planned. Her sister had an accident and couldn't go so Sam ended up going by herself. Looking back, she was glad she went. Even if it did leave her with piles of work.

Everything had been going great until the day their ship made a final port stop in Belize. Her plan had been to go cave tubing up in the rainforest that day. Little did she know that their tour group would be taken hostage en route to the cave. After several harrowing hours, many of which Sam spent desperately praying, they were miraculously rescued by the U.S. military – and Lee.

Sam smiled as she thought about Lee. She was attracted to him from the moment she set eyes on him, even though he had been very standoffish, almost rude. It wasn't until the last day of her vacation she found out why. He was working undercover to track down wanted criminals - who just so happened to be the ones that abducted her and others during their excursion.

After it was over and they had all been rescued, Lee and Sam spent her last evening in the city getting to know each other. They discovered they had a lot in common and both had grown up in small Midwestern towns.

As the evening ended, they exchanged numbers and Lee assured her once he was back in the States he would give her a call. She had heard from him exactly once - a very brief text message, telling her he was wrapping things up and would call her soon. She was beginning to wonder if he really was interested, after all...

Until now. Somehow this must have something to do with the abduction in Belize. But what could anyone possibly want with her? The whole idea made her more than a little jittery.

Looking back, she wished she had just told this detective to come to her office right then so she could get this over with!

The hands on the clock seemed to stop as the rest of the afternoon dragged on. She kept glancing at her phone but Lee never replied.

Finally it was 5:30 and time to go meet this mysterious Agent Donovan. She grabbed her coat and purse and headed to the elevator. As she punched the down button, she looked at her watch for the umpteenth time as she tapped her foot on the floor. The elevator was taking forever!

When she finally reached the first floor, the doors slid silently open. Sam peeked around before stepping out. Although she couldn't see anyone, she had a nagging feeling that eyes were following her and she suddenly had a strong urge to start running. Instead, she strode across the lobby as fast as her high-heeled shoes would allow.

Once outside, she stopped to collect her thoughts, shaking her head as if to clear it. *I am so paranoid these days.* With a quick look around, she impulsively decided to take a shortcut through the adjacent parking garage, knowing it would get her to the meeting place faster. It would also give her a chance to drop her briefcase off in her car.

When she got to the edge of the garage, she suddenly realized just how dark it was inside. Dark and isolated. She stood still for a minute as she peered inside, giving her eyes time to adjust to the lack of light. Before she could change her mind and head back the way she had just come, she forced herself to start walking, making a quick beeline for her car.

She breathed a sigh of relief when she got to her car. She glanced down at the keys in her hand and for a second, was tempted to jump inside and drive off - forget about meeting this Donovan character.

Just then, she saw something move out of the corner of her eye. She narrowed her eyes as she looked in that direction but couldn't make anything out. A slight shiver ran down her spine. She was **certain** she had seen something move. She tossed her bag in the car and quickly locked it.

Sticking to the outer edge of the garage, Sam made her way towards the exit door as fast as her legs would take her, telling herself the entire time that there was nothing to be afraid of – there was nothing there.

Soon, she rounded the corner of the garage – the exit door was in sight. She let out a sigh of relief.

Just as she put her hand on the knob, someone stepped out of the shadows and grabbed her from behind. She felt a sudden jolt of fear as a wet rag was shoved into her face.

Sam turned and twisted as she frantically fought to free herself from the ironclad grip that was around her waist. The rag that covered her nose and mouth reeking of strong chemicals. Within seconds, a fog circled her brain. She tried to scream but no sound would come out. As she slipped into unconsciousness, Sam whispered a name .... *Lee*.

The end.

The Story Continues...Download Book 2 (Winds of Deception) At <u>HopeCallaghan.com</u>

Made in the USA
Coppell, TX
21 May 2021

56091100R00090